Night Clouds

Domenico Corna

ISBN-10: 1481146483
ISBN-13: 978-1481146487

TO MY WIFE, MARIKA

CONTENTS

To all the dogs and cats
who have crowded our lives
with love

PART ONE

...up there on the upland

CHAPTER ONE

The day was so beautiful; some wind came down from the mountain. Perhaps it was spring or only its scent that from the high layers slipped into the valley. Large, white clouds floated in the sky like ships that, being detached from the port, begin their travel slowly, swinging, an enormous flock of sheep behind an invisible shepherd. Sometimes they joined; sometimes they were separated, following an instinct that Martina did not understand.

She looked up, taken away from the dynamics and their spell. Even her ears felt nothing but that slow sliding. In her head formed a sweet music—an unknown mental transport.

She closed her eyes and the clouds continued to slide in her thoughts, slowly. So she seemed to be in the middle of the clouds taking part of that gentle and tender walk.

The sky was so near and blue to seem everywhere, over and inside her head. It had a warm and sweet scent that seemed to push slowly and constantly from the wind. Martina spread her arms for a moment in an instinctive movement, following an illogical urge to catch the clouds.

An unexpected and uneasy feeling made a dark contrast in her mind that was impossible to define, and she began to gasp for breath, like after a long race.

It was not an apprehension or a real fear; it seemed instead the effect of the clouds' wake, as if they had as soon leave an disagreeable and distressing situation. A tense moment stirred her physical and mental state and made her heart race.

She did not know how much the white clouds and the heat of the sun had kidnapped her attention. She found herself sitting in a great, green meadow, with her back against a tree and her nose turned upward; what she had just seen and felt now was only a memory suggested in this moment.

#

Martina felt a great wish to keep crying; her eyes were moist, as she had just taken a break before resuming to cry. She felt wrapped in an inexplicable numbness. Her back was leaning against a large willow tree in the middle of a green meadow.

In front of her there was a white earth road furrowed with two parallels stripes like train tracks. In a middle of the road was a wide full green sod of crushed grass running like a third track.

The road unwound in wide curves between depressions and swellings of the land, as flowers bloomed from that fertile earth.

Her glance followed the road until a pine woods, a black spot where the sun could not enter. Only one beam from above infiltrated, piercing the dark, dense woods like a fire sword, illuminating the land like a projector on the scene of a movie.

Martina turned her head to look the other way; the road disappeared just beyond. So she thought she was on some part on a plateau.

Her breath was back to normal; she decided to get up. Her legs answered to hard work, as if they were raising an enormous weight. She grabbed the trunk of the tree to share her weight. Standing, she turned to look at the tree against which she had been leaning a little earlier. It was unusual the presence of a willow tree, which were accustomed to the humidity of the plains, on a plateau near pastures and pine woods.

The wind was blowing back her hair. She closed and opened her eyes, looking for something in her memory. She could not remember the reason for her presence: how she got here and what she was thinking before watching the clouds passing.

"Where am I?" she whispered slowly.

The sound of her voice seemed to alter the tranquility of the environment around her, as if an object were set down in the wrong place.

Lacking memory was a problem more serious than she had imagined.

She had lost much more than few seconds: back in time, could not find anything. Memory was an empty can—completely empty.

"Oh my God, what happened to me!" She passed her hand over forehead.

She did not remember anything: how she had come here and all the rest. Behind clouds all was disappeared.

She looked like she had sunk her hands into a bag, sure to find something that was just there. But no recent memory was inside, and each time her hands emerged full only of uncertainty and fear. Only her childhood could give her some faded pictures.

She knew who she was, how she lived her childhood, but the certainties stopped shortly after adolescence; after then, she did not remember anything.

Something serious must have happened…

She looked down at her legs, arms, hips, breasts, and touched her head and hair.

"I'm not so old! Nor shabby" she thought, taking the first steps on the road in the direction of the woods that were standing majestic as a mountain.

She walked slowly, looking around carefully, paying attention to everything. Perhaps if she had caught any small reference or recollection in her head, everything would resume the lost order, composing like a puzzle.

But more she looked around, the more she shook her head and spread her arms in a terrible feeling of helplessness.

"Maybe on a vacation," she thought, walking and looking around, "I came up here, and, running, I bumped my head somewhere, losing my memory. Of course it must have been so; it cannot be otherwise!"

She touched her head, looking for some confirmation of her hypothesis, but her head, like everything else, was in good condition.

"Now, behind the woods I will meet somebody and the nightmare will end. He'll tell me what really happened. I just need to get beyond the forest…"

It was only a short walk to the first pine trees.

"And if people were on the *other* side instead? If I were walking in the wrong direction…"

She slowed down, stopped, and, undecided and looking around, she listened, searching for familiar sounds. She spread her arms again, uneasy.

She wanted to scream for some help, but did not feel the necessary courage.

As she entered the woods and walked through the pines, the sun disappeared behind a wave of fresh branches, wrapped together with the intense scent of underbrush and fruitful humidity.

The woods were not very dense, with tall pines leaving space for low bushes and a brown carpet of almost-reddish, old, dry leaves of the past autumn. The sun crept among the branches, losing most of its light.

There was a great variety of birds and small rodents

running, immersed in their occupations, not at all scared by her presence.

It seemed that nobody lent her attention, not even out of fear for a foreign presence; she had to be careful where she put her feet to avoid crushing somebody.

She felt a brief hiss and a blow to the head. Something solid hit her then bounced on the ground. She bent down, picking up an acorn. She looked at it while she again put a hand to her head. She had been hit by an acorn, and, given the intensity of the blow, it could not have been falling from a tree. She peered around, looking for the culprit.

A squirrel from a nearby tree, after spying the effect of his wrongdoing, ran away and hid in a hole.

She remained for some time with the acorn in her hand, looking at the plant where the squirrel was gone. She wondered where acorns came from if there were only pine trees here. It was really a very strange place!

The sound of a brook stole her attention and also her doubts. A small river stood there, a little further on, foaming down between rock and moss.

Martina watched the water running, then chose two large stones to place in the water as steps or a bridge, and she easily crossed the river.

When she was on the other side, she took a look again to check if the squirrel still was around.

Everything was quiet now.

"If I am dead, have I ended up in some kind of earthly paradise?" she thought, stopping. There was also something humorous in this situation. Hit by acorns in paradise.

Maybe it was only a dream. Next morning, she would wake up sitting on her bed and remembering this place, the incredible feeling of presence, before resuming her normal day.

She thought how strange it felt to be becoming unknown to itself. Suddenly she didn't remember anything anymore: complete darkness on the events, the choices, the people who had meant something. All erased, as with a sponge.

Though she was walking slowly, the woods were soon behind her, and in front were other green hills softly and oh-so-slowly falling away.

On the right side stood a massive mountain. The wind carried thuds and through the dark as it slipped across a wide and deep scree as far as she could see.

Martina resumed her walking on the way down, bypassing the bumps. The slope began to increase, denying perspective. She could see only directly in front of her eyes. The trip turned into something like a run.

After some minutes she had an image of the horizon: there were lowlands hills rising from awkward and fat clouds, all somewhat blending together in the fog.

The hills had little definition, like mirages in the desert.

Between her and the hills on the horizon was interposed a long and endless prairie of arid and stringy vegetation. The heat distorted images, and the bushes moved, swaying in a slow dance. The dry land seems to be a huge expanse of water reflecting the sunlight—it looked like one of those American prairies populated by bison and wild horses. The vegetation consisted of very low bushes spaced apart. The only other plants were cactus like great fingers pointing to the sky.

Martina stopped her walk in disbelief at the sight. She looked back: the mountain was always still there, as was the dark sound of wind over the scree, as was the forest from which she had come. Her feet were still treading the fields whose consistency was more like that of expanses covered in moss.

So radical a change of nature could not be justified—so fast a transition from alpine vegetation to another semi-desert.

"What kind of place am I now?"

She, scratched her head slowly. There was no way for such a coexistence, two landscapes so different, with so strong a difference of weather. The fertile with the arid, dry climate with frequent rain. All so close to each other.

She passed the last green hills; down there it was an open space of beaten earth. Next, like a vision, a red and sloping roof of a house appeared. A pole came out from the corner; at the top there was a waving and cheerful flag flapping in the mountain wind.

"Thank God!" she thought.

"For sure, somebody lives there. This is a good news for my confused head!"

The thought came back to the willow and the clouds as she checked to see if at least those recent images were stored. She was able to perfectly reconstruct the events from that time until now.

"Whatever happened before, my head has started again to work!"

#

Martina, following the road, went up to the building with the red roof. She stopped in the large courtyard right in front. The house was shaped like a horseshoe: two separate buildings connected by a covered front porch. The road ended in the courtyard, and three small paths branched off in different directions.

A low fence, a little less than three feet tall, wrapped around the yard. It was formed by tree branches tied together with wire and nails, right as a mountain fence.

Beyond the fence began the endless prairie.

She still could not believe that strange union of forest and desert. The fresh breeze from the mountain, laden with pasture and pine-tree fragrance, mixed with hot and strong aromas coming from the prairie and dry land, as if the wind itself, in strange eddies, delighted in confusing her sense of smell.

The dark wood shutters and trim gave elegance to the house's exterior. Through a picture window she could see that a wooden staircase led to a mezzanine floor with a corridor.

On the ground floor there was a large door with a sign hanging above: Edi's Home.

"What a strange place!" she thought, looking around. She watched the yard, the house, the mountains, and the prairies.

"I wonder who lives here."

She was sure she had never been here before—and in the deep silence all around her, she felt like it was likely that no one had been there for a long time. After some hesitation, she decided to verify.

She slowly and carefully approached the door. At the door she paused to look at the very strange bell: it was a long rope, like the one that announces the beginning of functions in the church. At the upper end, the rope had been unraveled into many other smaller and different cords. There were many hanging pieces of wrought iron in the shapes of animals. The wind made them sway slowly, sometimes touching, producing an unreal sound that seemed to come from a wider area.

Martina pulled the cord, bringing together all the animals. A large amount of clinking spread all around.

She pulled a second time, waiting apprehensively, and was not sure whether to hope for someone's arrival.

After the second chime, a sound of footsteps was heard from inside. Shortly after appeared the smiling face of a woman with a large apron. Martina lost any apprehension. The woman was short and, like in a mirrors fun house, the lacking height appeared in the width of her flanks. But especially, Martina noted her smile: spontaneous and joyful; for sure she would help her.

"Good morning, Martina—welcome!"

The unexpected greeting from the woman surprised the girl and stopped her any other consideration. She looked around, wondering if there was ever any other Martina.

"Excuse me, but—do you know me?"

The woman seemed surprised at such a question. "Of course I know you—you're Martina!"

The girl nodded but watched the woman with curiosity and suspicion.

"Is something wrong with you?" the woman asked, and she smiled.

"No, no! I think not, it's okay! I only have a little confusion in my head, but it's okay!"

"Confusion?" asked the woman, surprised.

"Yes, I think I have some kind of amnesia."

A contracted face further accentuated Martina's expression. "I don't even remember who you are."

The woman smiled.

"It's been a long time. It's understandable you do not remember me. My name is Ginetta; I am Edi's mother!" She put a particular emphasis on *Edi*. Martina still looked at the woman with curiosity. "Really—we know each other?"

"Of course, from a long time ago. Edi did not believe you'd come back, but I said, 'You'll see; soon she will be back!' So now, here you are!" She opened her arms emphatically, as to welcome Martina's having come back.

"I'm sorry, but I can't join your joy; I completely lost my memory—I don't remember ever being up here. I have such a mess in my head" said Martina, putting her hands on her forehead. "I forgot everything! Who I am, who I was, what I did in my life. I keep only some memories about childhood."

Ginetta smiled with wide-open eyes; she seemed to struggle to restrain a great emotional urge to hug the girl. She seemed only to be waiting for a nod from Martina for permission to show her joy.

Martina would have this affection—that round and nice face!—but the woman was a stranger to her, and she did not feel like hugging her.

She looked down, and Ginetta understood her reticence; she changed her demeanor but not her smile.

"I'm really glad you're here again; you'll see, everything will work out, and you'll have back your memory, I'm sure! Meanwhile, it is better have a little rest; I have prepared your usual room—"

"My usual room?" interrupted Martina.

"Of course, your favorite room. All the times you're up here, you've always wanted the same room."

"I've been long here?"

"Oh yes! There was a time when you did not want down anymore; you said this was your world, and you just wanted to stay here forever."

Ginetta looked back again at Martina. "But really you do not remember?"

Martina shook her head. "I do not remember anything about all the things you are telling me and who knows how many other."

"Do not worry; everything's gonna be okay."

Martina nodded with a smile. "But—for the payment? I just don't have any money with me," she said, putting her hands in her pockets.

Ginetta smiled, amused. "Don't worry! It's all already paid in advance—from *a long time*!"

Martina could not understand.

"From a long time," said Ginetta, still smiling wistfully.

#

They crossed the courtyard and climbed the wooden staircase to the first floor. They climbed, silently except a slowly creaking the polished floorboards.

They went into the hall, and Ginetta opened the door of the first room. "Here we are, this is the room! Do you like it?"

Martina smiled and went inside, but the contrast with the strong external light made the room dark; without checking, she replied affirmatively.

With a smile, Ginetta handed her the keys and went

back into the hallway. "Keep your time; here, you can take all the time you want."

The door closed, leaving Martina alone in gloom. She waited for moment, then went to one of the two windows.

The shutters creaked, opening; the wind hit Martina on the forehead and blew back her hair. She turned around to look at the whole room and just smiled.

The four walls were covered with drawings of dogs and cats of all shapes and colors and in all possible attitudes: dogs eating, running, and even peeing. Cats sneaked behind bushes or slept on straw chairs.

The ceiling was full of clouds: drawn clouds with noses, eyes, and expressions of wonder. They had some features in common with the clouds Martina had seen near the willow tree.

"What an odd place," she whispered, looking at the drawings.

She went back to the window and rested her arms on the windowsill that faced the mountain. Pushed by the wind, inside came a pleasant smell of grass and undergrowth.

On the opposite side there was another window; Martina went in that direction and opened two shutters and was impressed by a sight so out of the ordinary: an endless prairie undulating in the heat from the ground.

Maybe because of the immensity of the prairie or the limitless vista, something moved in her head—feelings impossible to define. Excitation so strong, she felt the desire to run away until she reached the low hills on the horizon.

It was the imagination calling Martina to let herself go: close her eyes and run without limits on a inviting prairie, bright, near and far, timeless. Those profiles of vegetation so brave to adapt to the dry land, taken care of by heat and haze, an intense aroma seemed to arise from nowhere, bringing with it the feeling of eternity.

Martina's thinking was behaving as if she were back

home and, out of happiness, she would run up and down into the prairie.

Her mind was much larger than the body that surrounded it; an irrepressible force urged her to set her body aside, close her eyes, and let go.

Martina was scared, wondering if this urge was of the same power that had wiped her past from her mind as a load too heavy to bring along.

Her mind's impulse was running fast, involving her lungs. Her heart began beating faster and her breath stumbled. It was all too powerful to be compressed into a small body.

She was scared; she opened her eyes looked down, and checked her breath. It was the same breathlessness feeling she had had near the willow when she was watching the clouds.

Now she was sure something was wrong in her head. It was too dependent on external feelings; a place so dry and sunny had the strength to penetrate her mind and carry away her thoughts.

"I'm too tired now to understand."

She waited with apprehension for her breathing to return back to normal. She was puzzled!

"It's really a strange place!"

#

The sun was still hot when Martina slowly came out of the room and went down the stairs, slowly, being careful to prevent any noise. She left the courtyard behind without looking back; she did not want other oddities from Ginetta. She passed the fence and dropped down to the prairie.

The ground was hard and dry; there were stringy and sharp bushes, low and curved, like the profile of unhappy people who complained of their ungrateful fate to be there.

The prairie was the image of a perpetual struggle for life; Martina seemed fascinated by the courage coming from that land. The struggle for life gave to those dry shrubs an eternal dimension.

There were no trails around; no one passed before her.

The sun was very hot, the cicadas pushed their singing from bush to bush, far away. Intense flavors came to her nose.

She turned, looking to the other side: the green pastures and woods, where the climate was so different. The shelter seemed a crib set at the beginning of the mountain. She walked into the prairie, wondering if her mind's instinct to run away was a natural predisposition, or a sort of dependence on external factors.

Perhaps it had happened other times.

Maybe, whenever the mind went away, it carried off all the memories.

Perhaps it had happened also up there, beside the willow tree—she had yielded to a mind, a little too much enterprising, that had carried away her memories and left her emptied.

If it was really true there was no escape!

Perhaps now, unknowingly, was under some impulse of her mind, the fact of being in a place so strange was the demonstration of a mind that was walking away right now, right here.

Perhaps, awakening, she would start again from zero.

#

The evening was slowly coming down from the mountain, along the prairie to the far hills, when Martina was back to Ginetta; she had prepared dinner and made Martina sit at an old wooden table.

The girl told her about her walk down into the plain. "It's a very strange place! We are only one step from a big mountain in the middle of woods, meadows so green they dazzle the eyes, and, just a few meters down, there are desert bushes and dead branches, with the sun so strong that it seems always near to burning everything.

"Even animals behave in a strange way; there was a squirrel in the woods who liked to throw the acorns against me."

Ginetta was smiling. "It's just because of that, why you liked so much to come here. You said that there was no place in the world more beautiful."

Martina was looking at the woman with a little suspicion. She was waiting for a moment before asking a difficult question.

How can ask a dream if it is real?

"But is it true, what I'm living now, or am I dreaming or hallucinating?"

Ginetta smiled again calmly. "What's the difference?"

"Of course it makes a difference. I want to know if my life is after I wake up, or if this is my life!"

"Me too; I often wonder if this is my life, or just a dream. But it is not very important; I live here, and there is no better world for me!"

Martina watched every gesture, every word, that strange smile whose meaning she could not sense. She felt Ginetta's smile was like the smile of somebody hiding a pleasant surprise in the next room—a birthday gift, maybe—and just waiting for the right moment to bring out the surprise.

"I'm sure, you'll get the missing memories; you must have faith. Sometimes something strange happens that causes loss of memory, and then you feel lost, but the memory at last can find an opening and go back."

Ginetta was going to the kitchen; the phrase trailed off beyond the door.

She came back shortly after, carrying two steaming plates that she put on the table, and they began to eat together. Martina was spying on all her actions, carefully but secretly watching everything Ginetta did. "I bet you know something about all the oddities in my head, do you not?"

Ginetta, bowing her head, smiled at the girl's provocation. "Once I knew everything about you: I could guess your thoughts, your movements—but it was a long time ago. Now I'm not so sure; you look so changed!"

Martina did not know what to say.

"I have no doubt about your memory coming back! But I don't know how will happen and how long it will take. Meanwhile you'll be here with me! If you want, this place will get into your head and make you understand how important is fantasy and the imagination"

Ginetta smiled; Martina was listening carefully.

"This is not a place like any other. The woods, the meadows, and the mountains are not only forests, grassland and mountains!

"This is the closest place to the heart; it is the mirror, and, if you want to look inside, will take you far, far beyond your normal possibilities."

The woman's eyes were bright with an inner light.

"The Martina I knew ran so fast, her fantasy was so strong to as to leave behind nature. I watched her every sunset leaning against the fence, pushing the sight down to the prairie. I saw her, into the night, overcome and move away, slowly following an instinct that I could not understand."

The woman seemed strange, gently remembering the times when she was with her.

"Don't be in a hurry to bring back your memory; let it return without haste. Do not be afraid! If only you knew how important it is for the imagination to run free!

"Don't go around looking for bits of the past, their fears bulky and heavy as boulders. Think about the great opportunity to stand here, and don't inhibit thoughts.

"Let your mind run free!"

CHAPTER TWO

The willow tree was still up there on the upland; there was some doubt Martina had about it. She left in the morning, together with Ginetta.

The woman had reluctantly agreed to the climbing effort; she hard panted, and took long and frequent breaks, leaning on a stick.

The girl seemed rather invigorated, and urged the woman with continuous questions. When they reached the upland, Martina pointed to the tree of the earliest memory and Ginetta had a long sigh of relief and sank into the grass, her back to the trunk, and waited the breath be normal.

Even the girl lay down against the willow tree, on the opposite side. She stared at the sky, which brought to mind the day before's impressions. She spoke slowly, with long pauses, sometimes closing her eyes to better compare the previous day's memories.

"Even today, the clouds seem to behave the same way. Like yesterday they are so fascinating. They go from one to another part of the sky as if to follow a precise fate. They meet and leave each other, immersed in their own dimension, so close that they seem alive. If you look carefully, after a while, they seem to be enraptured by their own dynamism. Navigate with them!" Martina paused, with a deep sigh.

"Who knows how long I have been there to watch? One minute, an hour, a day, or maybe more. I thought I had lost the sense of time. Perhaps there is no time," she said, pointing to the sky.

Ginetta also turned her eyes upward, carefully watching while she listened.

"If I look away, it has had a tearing effect, a sudden awakening. I realized that had forgotten all about my life, all except for a few details regarding my childhood, just enough to know who I am. I was scared—maybe something happened to me. I also thought I was dreaming; perhaps nothing around me was real, so I waited until everything disappeared like in a dream."

A breath of wind came down from the mountain; Martina paused, turning her face to enjoy the fresh air.

"I've waited for a long time, but the clouds were still always running, and I still do not remember why I was there. I can't explain; in that moment it was like born again! Without identity…" She spread her arms with sadness.

"But then, logic here does not seem to be at home! Is there any logic in a semi-desert prairie next to alpine meadows, divided only by a small shelter?" She pointed in the direction the refuge. Ginetta smiled.

"I even thought myself to be a cloud falling down into a place like heaven!"

Ginetta smiled again.

"I also thought I was a victim of some disease. Confined in some closed and protected park…" She turned to Ginetta, watching the woman's reaction. "It's not that true I'm really in some mental hospital and you're checking my madness?"

Ginetta turned to her again, looking stern. Martina did not wait for the woman's reply, shrugged her shoulders, it was plausible to think also this possibility.

Martina began to look at the clouds, but the smile faded slowly to sadness. "What do you think about? I don't know my character. I just feel scared! I'm worried—"

"I don't remember that you were so complicated!" interrupted Ginetta. "Why do you worry so much about the past? The past is just a moment like so many. What do you care if seems to be disappeared? Sooner or later it will come back. Instead, you should be pleased for an open mind, without a lot of weight on you."

"But I can't live without knowing who I was before!"

Martina turned to look at Ginetta, who, instead of responding, remained quiet, seemingly indifferent to the girl's problems.

In the silence between their words, there was only the sound of the leaves touching each other under the wind's breath. The clouds still were flowing and Martina, watching, tried to hold back the following instinct: a strange invitation to free her mind from any other thought. She turned her eyes away when she realized the imminent danger.

Ginetta smiled but was sad in spite of her gesture. "You're so different! How much you're changed; it is sad, watching, to discover that you are afraid. It never happened before! See, you look away and avoid your imagination, just to keep a handful of small memories."

The woman sighed, shaking slowly the head. "I'm really sad, following your words. The Martina I knew when she coming here, did not bring anything with her. The sad thoughts, worries, and fears were not able to follow her. Looking at her, I understood her emotions, her happiness."

She had a nostalgic smile.

"When you arrived here, it was a holiday. It was like in the morning when the sun comes up; you were so dynamic, it was impossible not to be infected. You told me, with a smile: 'How much I would to stay here forever.'"

Ginetta sighed again, with an absent look and smiling. "Like the time your eyes were popping out; you came running up from that road." She stretched out her arm to the downhill road in the opposite direction from where they had come. "You were so happy, and your eyes so shined, to want at all costs I come down with you to see. I couldn't refuse."

"What's down there?" Martina asked.

The woman, deep in thought, seemed not to hear Martina's request.

"You said, 'I'm going to think about it! There, the thoughts run faster.'"

"Don't want tell me what's over there?" Martina was curious. The woman smiled.

"Why I should say? To deprive you of the pleasure to find out? If you really want to find out what's out there, all you have to do is go! Follow the path, you will find a piece of your past; is not that what you're looking for?"

Martina looked at the woman and then the road.

"What are you waiting for?" urged Ginetta. "I have breathing problems; I can't follow you."

Martina got up and took a few steps on the road; then she turned to look at her, was not sure if Ginetta was joking.

"Go!" Ginetta smiled pointing the way. "I'll be here waiting for you, like many times before, when you came running to tell me everything!"

#

The road descended slowly, into a dense forest, full of old pine needles, tall and slender trunks nearly touching the clouds, which were imposing as old men with white holiday hats.

A large quantity of birds flew, pressing into the top of the sky and calling to each other.

The path was crossed transversely by strong roots that consolidated the patchy and uneven ground like a drawing in relief. Martina jumping lightly over roots, thinking about the reason for so much mystery. Would not it make more sense if Ginetta had revealed what was down here? Martina had other troubles to think about.

The path winded down, the wind increased, and pine trees thinned out to make space for other, different pines, another species, lower and grayer. Disappeared also was the intense humid undergrowth, and large flowering shrubs began to adorn the path like a garden. In the air was a large mix of perfumes; there was one in particular that Martina could isolate but could not define; it reminded her of childhood. She was unable to recollect what generated that scent.

After she walked down for a few minutes, the forest began to reduce; in between the remaining gray pines was left much space, occupied by reduced vegetation. There were flowering shrubs and low creepers on the ground.

The trail finally came out in a large meadow uphill whose perspective leading the eye to the clouds. She could not see or imagine what lay beyond, but she was sure she had arrived at her destination.

Flocks of birds sailed the sky making noise; they were flying high and then would swoop down, disappearing behind the strange, forced horizon.

The air was dense with the scent that may have upset her memory previously. Under the impulse of curiosity, Martina took the last steps, until the strange perspective vanished like a curtain rising.

A loud and immense noise came to her ears; her eyes uncertainly began to transfer to her mind the images in front of her.

"I can't believe it; there is also the sea in this place!"

Right in front of her, the cliff formed a promontory,

coming uphill along the line of the sea for a hundred yards.

Martina walked slowly on the strip of land until she reached where the path ended as if she were standing on the bow of a ship. The sea beneath her was calm but crashed foaming on the rocks.

"How can I have forgotten a place like this?"

She was scared, sat on top of the hill, the last piece of land before the blue of the sky and the sea.

"If only I could remember!"

The cape seemed to go right into the sea, as a bridge to another dimension.

Martina got up to look around. It had to be the right place where usually she stopped, where thoughts run fast, as Ginetta had told her.

The sky and the horizon had the same blue intensity. The sound of the sea, and the waves drowned out any other noise; only the gulls with their calls were able to compete as they swooped down to the sea, passing close to the promontory, just a little away from her, then continued down to the water's surface, only to turn again upward.

She seemed to be like one of them, hanging in the air without a secure grip—without certainties.

Again her thoughts pushed her to let go, to be ready to change with her imagination what her eyes were seeing. Martina was distracted and did not realize she was losing control. The deep blue sky, a painting with pastel colors, turned above her. Her eyes closed slowly under the impulse of the wind. Her lips widened in a smile, and her arms were stretched as if to take flight, with the intention of following the wind.

She felt the sensation of a swallow ready for its first flight; she needed only a little push to get closer to the clouds. At each turn the wings and wind would support her in the desired direction.

She could rise high, working her muscles hard then surrendering to inertia. She would sit on the wind, motionless, suspended in the air, waiting for a moment before falling wildly. Out of control, she would feel the wind move her from all sides. She would wait for the right moment to stretch her wings just a little, feel the wind again slowly start to support her, and, when the wind speed decreased, spread suddenly her right wing in an abrupt left turn.

She would fly gently in the air like a Sunday morning quiet walk.

She was slowly getting closer to the lower clouds, getting inside, feeling their fresh caress, and immediately she emerged on the opposite side, where the sun was ready to heat her. Moving clouds with one wing, she change their direction. Challenging the gulls to climb higher, she nosedived down until she was just a few feet above the beach, until she quickly shifted midair and flew even higher than before, without any vertigo feeling.

Martina, absorbed by her feelings, her mind completely absent, followed her imagination without noticing. Thoughts multiplied, amplifying these sensations. She seemed to be in the middle of a thousand emotions. As a child suddenly arrived in Toyland, she could not refrain from touching and trying everything.

She was stunned by the variety of her insight.

Martina suddenly left her airborne transport and found herself on a train platform. It was an old station on an early autumn day, and two tracks sank into the fog just as they seemed to join.

The morning fog was, gradually dissolving, lengthening the perspective.

She was sitting on an old bench that was green and rust-chewed, and she was feeling a strange, persistent sensation, as if she had been waiting for someone for a long, long time—perhaps forever.

Constantly said to herself, "It will be here soon!" From the fog would appear a figure. Finally she would get up to meet someone.

But weariness was holding her, the fear of not being

able to maintain this long waiting. She could get up and go away—give up. Only a thought kept her from such decision: "Maybe it's getting here right now. From the mist I'll see the figure come along!"

Martina was impressed; the scene looked like a nightmare. She left in a hurry to move over a large green field of grass. She ran barefoot on the freshly cut grass, over groves meticulously chamfered. She ran at breakneck speed, sometimes closing her eyes and opening her arms, and sometime suddenly stopping and starting, like a colt long kept in the barn.

She felt a sense of freedom shake her soul down in every part of her body, like a lifeline. She laughed in a long happiness, deep and immense.

"Martina!" There was somebody beside her—a baby! He was sullen, looking at her; he stopped, because he could not run faster; he was resting his hands on his knees and panting.

He asked her to stop running in that way. Martina laughed, looking at the child gasping with exhaustion; she laughed again, even happier.

"Don't run so fast; I can't keep up with you. Wait for me!"

Maybe it was the feeling of running barefoot or lawns or sunny day or a friend who asked to follow, or all things together, but Martina was happy.

Suddenly the meadow, the sky, and the clouds disappeared to give way to an arid prairie, full of dry shrubs. She walked slowly towards the low hills at the meadow's end. The wind had abruptly created a vortex and quickly increased its strength.

A dust cloud began to envelop her; she put her hands over her eyes to protect herself. She felt lifted into the air.

Opening her eyes, she saw there was no more dust around her; she was sitting on the top of a vortex that was flowing around her as if she sat in the palm of its hand. The vortex took a tornado structure and moved swung across the ground rising a big dust cloud. Martina was breathless, and her heart was near bursting for the emotion.

The child was down on the ground with his hands on his hips and his face dark with anger, beating down his feet in the dust so she would notice him.

"Ugh! I want me also on the tornado; why always you can and not me? Every time I have to wait down here! Come on, let me go up!" A moment later both rode the tornado as if it were a young horse to tame.

"Hold on tight, because now we dance!" said Martina.

Round the prairie echoed the cries of fear and happiness of the two children.

The image faded to give way to another. The child faded too, but none took his place.

There still was the prairie, but it was night-time. Strange, phosphorescent clouds lit up the sky from the horizon to its zenith. She was sitting, her upturned nose following the clouds' movements. Her face was attentive; her eyes were changing expression and her brows were shifting as if she were listening to somebody telling stories. She has sometimes smiling, and sometimes sad. The clouds were moving around her, lowered, falling down to brush her face. Then, when the story seemed finished, they came back up. Martina held out her hand to make them fall again. The clouds made a wide circle after lowering again, floating and illuminating her face.

Another time the image of the prairie faded away like an echo bounced many times in the mountains.

The image changed to give way to the silence; somebody was in a middle of the woods, slowly coming down. She could feel the smell of vegetation and the birds singing in the tops of pine trees. Her mind was full of doubts. She was wondering what was going on and where she was going now.

She got down slowly, step by step, until she reached a meadow which denied the viewing. The last minutes she passed in anxious waiting. She felt a strange smell but did not understand its source until she was standing in front of it.

She had come to the sea! In front there was a boundless stretch of water.

Martina gasped and opened her eyes, cutting off suddenly her imagination. The last dream was about her, only few minutes before; just when she was descending the mountain. For a moment it seemed an ancient thought, intense and exciting as the others. It was instead a strong emotion stored with the beach with all the others.

Her heart began to pound.

#

Ginetta was dozing, leaning on a willow tree, waiting for her.

Martina arrived and explained what had happened—the strange memories that suddenly had come inside her head.

Ginetta smiled, listening.

"How many times I have dreamed to hear you speak again like this! Waiting, as before, for your return, so I might hear the imagination stories. But even more at night!"

Ginetta closed the eyes. "The night was a time when collected dreams fall down to you like fruit from a tree. You had said that thoughts become real when the night clouds appear and make you fly like a kite in the sky. Then the intuition has no limits; dreams become visible and cover themselves with lights, memories, and images. How many times I have asked myself if the day has come to hear you in the same way?"

She had a long sigh, then her face became sad. "How can you say now to be afraid—just you! You, whose fear was only when thought could not leave the ground and forced you to have only normal feelings."

Martina was even more confused.

"How can I not be afraid? All my past is a mystery! I have a terrible loneliness and empty feeling! When I think about it, I wonder if I had had some friend, maybe the love of a boy. I lost everything—"

"What do you remember from your childhood, your dreams?" Ginetta interrupt.

"Childhood?" Martina thought about her childhood—how to interpret a young age, ways of thinking, a child's wishes, how to understand for could tell the joys and fears? She was no longer a child and could not understand how to recall a child's life.

"I remember I was a difficult little girl; my parents didn't know how to behave with me. I saw my father worried when he came home from work. I knew most of his concerns regarded me."

Ginetta listened silently as Martina continued.

"I felt an overwhelming need to play in a way that nobody could understand. I often went out alone; I spoke with dogs and cats. My mother said I was too sensitive; I couldn't live in this world without adequate protection. When autumn came, I would start crying if I saw the trees next to the ditch behind the house become dry. I collected their leaves, bringing those home to keep warm, gently stroking. Maybe someone returned green and I hung on to the tree for life again.

"When the bad days followed, and the sky remained gray from morning till evening, I was afraid for the sun; perhaps he had lost his way back to our country. I stood outside the house, waiting for his appearance. I sometimes secretly left the lights on all night, so the sun could see them and find the way back to us."

Martina turned to Ginetta, and they both smiled.

"How many dogs have I made crazy with my obsessions! I stopped them from talking. They followed me home as if I were a Pied Piper."

The woman smiled; Martina hesitated.

"For my parents thought it very strange to see me

spend so much time in that way. If an ant climbed on the chair, I entertained for a long time to talk to her; I followed her journey with my index finger. I discovered where she came from and where she was going."

Martina laughed, remembering her childhood.

"My parents thought I was a little crazy, and I could not blame them, but it was an instinct that I could not escape. I became sad when I realized that I could not understand the gestures or expressions of anything near to me. I seemed to lose something very important and unique!"

Martina's voice became soft.

"This was my world; my friends looked at me with suspicion. How do you go around a small town with somebody whose main entertainment is talking to the dogs? Their parents took them away from me, admonishing them to seek other friendships. My parents were worried and could not understand why I didn't behaved like all the other children and find common interests. In the start they were waiting, sure that my crazes soon would be gone. Then they lost all hope, went the hard way, and decided to punish me!"

Her face became dark.

"A kind of punishment like a nightmare. For two hours every afternoon for a week, I would be locked up in the dark in the broom closet, the only place in the house I was scared. Only thinking about that closet had always given me the creeps. I figured there was something or someone hidden there, ready to jump out if only I lingered to watch. I passed by on the run from the door, keeping my eyes fixed ahead for fear that someone could hang my gaze. I pleaded for them to reconsider; I swore firmly, promising not to speak with the dogs. I would go with my friends to play their games. But my pleading had no effect; I had to get in the closet. It was a terrible punishment; the closet was dark and narrow, and I was so scared…"

Martina waited for a moment; the memories still hurt.

"I was scared and crying. I was hoping they were soon to get me out. The minutes seemed eternal; my heart was pounding, and I hid my face in my hands. I wanted to cry out, loudly, shouting till they came to the door."

Ginetta smiled at her story; her eyes became bright.

"Then, after some time, I also learned to speak with the people. We moved to the city, I started to go to school—"

Martina stopped suddenly.

"All the rest is unknown to me!"

CHAPTER THREE

The evening had fallen at the farm; Martina stood, leaning against the fence and watching the sunset. For her, the sun went down for the second time, leaning on the back of the hills. She felt sad, even had spent a beautiful day with Ginetta.

She talked for a long time about her childhood, hoping the old memories, and also the newer ones, would return later. But it was useless; her memories mercilessly stopped at the beginning of adolescence as if curtain had dropped early, after only the first act.

Leaning on the fence, she was watching the last rays of the sun as the clouds roamed the prairie. A sadness and loneliness enveloped everything; maybe there was a truth hidden somewhere, but eluded her.

How long she remain here, locked in this earthly paradise, before she knew who she was and where she should go? How far was she from her house, if she ever had one? And friends? She wondered if some friends were still looking for her. She had memories about some friends, but everything turned off, like all the rest, at the start of adolescence, when she had moved to the city.

Martina had lived in a small town a few miles away from the city. Every morning she had to take the bus to go to school. She did not like to go to the city. She liked the countryside and the mountains surrounding her like a hug. In the morning, opening the window, it looked those mountains were there for her, having waited all night.

In springtime, when some thunderstorm had shaken the night and the wind flowed across the plain with a long hissing, the mountains seemed near her hands, cleaned again, wearing a holiday dress.

She was badly impressed by the city, the traffic, the people, the sad faces running around, the people bumping into each other. The trees planted on the streets looked so sad! Even her mother, coming into town, took on a sad face; she would begin to walk as fast as everyone else, nervously pulling Martina by the hand. So Martina thought it was the city that make people sad and nervous.

She liked only the big orange bus; it shook on rough roads as if she was in a rocking chair. Those buses crawled through the narrow lanes with unimaginable agility.

Her memories stopped after the first few school years.

Martina was leaning on the fence, watching the prairie; the confusion of the city was so far away from a place so harmonious.

The sun had gone down behind the low hills. Only a halo was still leaning over the hilltops. She stood for a long time to observe the flow of colors from red to all possible mutations, before the colors were lost in the dark. Meanwhile, she thought thinking of her situation, her sadness, and the possible countermeasures to be taken. But the thoughts must have seemed devoid of time, as she realized that the red glow did not decrease in intensity. Instead, the shades seemed to brighten with on an unreal light, making long, red streaks on the contours of the hills.

"What a strange light" she whispered in disbelief. She

looked around for the strange light's source, but the farm, mountains, and forests on the plateau were completely dark.

Her gaze, fueled by curiosity, returned to the low hills and to the weird light. She wanted to find out what it was, but it was too far to get there—too much walking into the dark in the middle of a unknown prairie. She didn't feel the courage to climb over the fence and set off in that direction.

"This will probably be one of the many oddities of this place." she whispered, but her curiosity did not abate as she stared at the strange, red streaks.

Their reflections were like some of the most beautiful sunsets when, after a time, only the last clouds remain reflecting, like a mirror, the light of the sun—very tall clouds, thin streaks of ice while the sky is dark.

Even the prairie, in that light, changed its colors in a succession of slow and dynamic flare. Like a thunderstorm flashes, the strange red streaks approached and even illuminating what had been the dark portion of the sky near the farm.

The lights looked like musical notes: a huge flock of musical notes in ascending and descending scales, forming a melody.

She wanted to go over the fence, but did not feel the courage to take risks; the dark frightened her, just like when she was a little girl in the broom closet.

She clenched her fists. "I have to go!—I can't not find out what is it. I will take only a few minutes; I'll be careful where I put my feet!"

She jumped, over the fence and walked into the prairie.

Ginetta, at the window, had followed the whole scene; when Martina climbed over the fence to join the prairie, Ginetta smiled, and her eyes brightened.

#

Martina walked on the prairie for a few minutes, her heart pounding. She was trying to drive away every sensations of danger by looking only at the ground just in front of her.

The air was warm, slipping low around the flavors of bushes, the scent of the flowers stolen only a few moments before they would close for the night.

Many times Martina stopped to calculate the distance traveled; if the way she chose would be enough, and was it time to go back. But every minute the prairie lit up with the red flashes of the continuous light waves.

Her eyes moved from the ground to the sky, which seemed close enough now for a better look. There were clouds, strange clouds, constantly moving like a bonfire with different movements of many flames climbing from the base of the fire. Some flames seemed to disappear soon after their birth; others were projected very far, shining, like a bright light, across the entire prairie. It looked like a huge display of fireworks. Martina walked to the middle of the prairie in this surreal light.

She stopped when she seemed to be at the center of the light's dynamism. From there, the flashes departed, dispersing in a perfect circle into all points of the sky.

She had come to the source, though nothing could identify it—not a stone or a strange hole came from that strange energy, only other bushes.

Martina sat down; her fear was gone behind the charm of such a spectacle. The sky was throbbing red, and the silence was full of sensations, such when nighttime lightning announces a distant storm and the mysterious silence is charged with electricity, and the night seems to stop, waiting for the first thunder.

"Night clouds! These must be night clouds" she whispered, thinking about Ginetta's words, up there on the upland, about strange clouds that make the imagination live.

The clouds began to fall, at first slowly and timidly, as if to study her reaction.

Martina controlled every movement. She could hear the clouds, and almost touch them and feel their consistency, like breath that takes shape in a cold day.

The first cloud touched her face; there were images inside, floating softly, as if enclosed in a huge soap bubbles. The clouds hovered, approaching with discretion, and then went away slowly.

After gently touching her head, this image of clouds slipped away, leaving Martina a little confused. Her eyes followed the image's wake. This impression was like a distant music on a windy day; as if a bizarre wind carried the faraway melody to her ears, making it seem closer.

A cloud came back to touch her, then another lowered; the images inside were multiplied.

Martina followed these images until they projected inside her head. Behind the push of these images the night and the prairie began to disappear.

Shortly she was completely submerged.

#

There was the image of a city inside; somebody was walking on a sidewalk.

It was her city. She recognized the downtown streets, the square, the bus stop and the people waiting. It was a bright day, perhaps around noon; people were getting off the bus impatiently.

She was just the girl walking on the sidewalk, younger, the school books under her arm. Lost in thoughts, she was wearing a brown sweater with drawings and nodes.

Suddenly Martina remembered the occasion: it was her fifteenth birthday; her mom had given her that sweater as a gift for an important day. She could hear those thoughts as if she were thinking them now, with the same intensity.

As a revelation, that period of life opened in her mind. Her childhood had been over from a long time, and something had changed: she was no more in the country, and she could exchange no words with dogs. She had become curious about the city and its boys, especially the ones around the central square.

They sat around the fountain or on low walls of the square in a strange loneliness, though they were neighbors and close together. They had like thoughts and looks. If somebody passed near, they showed contempt, like a pack of wolves ready to defend themselves.

They could be seen, at any time of the day or night, migrating from the main square to the adjacent streets, beyond the smaller squares, to the gardens at the edge of the historic center.

Her mom had always recommended to avoid them and not talk with them. Their attitudes, her mom had told her, indicated a strange disease, the one without any remedy. All of them would die in a short time.

That day, Martina had decided to disobey.

Her thought came back many times to the square, imagining herself to be one of them; she liked that attitude that was a bit scruffy, even disdainful; that gaze at passers-by gave her a strange excitement.

She would have liked to stay with them and talk freely, playing and singing without caring about anything.

She had resisted many times the temptation to approach them, but she was not part of their world. She could not approach in the square and ask, "Excuse me, how do I get into your group?"

She made a promise to herself, abandoning any indecision; on her fifteenth birthday, she would sit around the fountain in front of all the boys. She would have done anything to get noticed.

So she convinced her mom to buy that unusual and different sweater for an important occasion.

#

Martina had arrived in the square, after having walked to its edge and back several time, each time bracing herself against the urge to leave and not go back, and each trip stopping in front of all the store windows. After a clothing shop, a wicker store, a wedding favors boutique, and an ice cream shop, she came finally to the beginning of the square, there was nothing else around to use as a pretext for hesitation.

In the center of the square, the boys talked to each other. A second group was a bit apart. A strange guitar sound bounced around the walls. A few white puffs of smoke, like signal, rose up from the center of the group. Martina went to sit down on the stone under the edge of the fountain at a certain distance. She kept her head down, only sometimes looking up to check the boys' movements.

The group was in a circle as if to protect a ritual that was taking place inside. People waiting for the bus watched the boys with contempt and went away shaking the heads.

Martina smiled. Her smile, as bait, met one boy's gaze. He was looking in her direction and pointed her out to the others. Other gazes turned in the same direction.

Martina felt lost; her heart was pounding when one of the boys, breaking away from the others, came up to her. She wanted to run away.

"I've never seen before; are you new here?"

Martina's eyes were firmly on the ground; she turned red like a watermelon, and could not answer that question.

The boy, however, was perfectly at ease, looking at her as at an old friend.

"It's not that you're a little fused?"

She thought, "Fused? What did he mean by *fused*?"

Although she had some difficulty speaking with them, she certainly was no moron. "No! I'm not... fused!"

"I understand! Then you're new here!"

Martina looked up, saw the quiet smile of the boy, and relaxed. She nodded knowingly, as if their simple exchange were a sin. The boy began to laugh.

"Look! Nobody will hurt you if you come!"

He suggested she follow; without answering, Martina stood up and walked to the other boys.

They widened the circle just a little, so she could be a part of it. Someone said hello; some other did not note her presence. She sat down on the ground like the others and remained silent.

A strange cigarette passed from hand to hand; each person took a puff, than passed it to the next person. When her time came, Martina looked it carefully and then immediately passed it on.

All the boys smiled briefly.

Martina's look went beyond the circle; people waiting for the bus were watching, and some shook their heads. She felt pride, had realized the purpose and it was not so hard.

PART TWO

…down here in the city

CHAPTER FOUR

It was dark all around when Martina took control of her thoughts. The night clouds were suddenly raised. The prairie silence contrasted with the animation in her head. Slow to fade away were the traffic images, the people in the square, and the colors of the afternoon.

Martina was sitting on a rock, waiting for the thoughts from the square to return to her like recalcitrant sheep that in the evening should get back into the fold.

The prairie seemed even more a place without dimension, without limit; the bushes were imperfect forms floating on a huge lake like a slow, imperceptible flow of dark algae.

Instinctively, a feeling of fear rose as she was breaking away from the square; it was a deep concern and disconcerting, to see that girl in the square so different from the small Martina dreamer.

She would ever remember that from that moment, her life was changed. In a few months she had moved to the square, at the beginning running away just a little from lessons, but eventually, all her interests had moved there.

Finally she left the school.

So it was definitely over, her childhood; the imagination that had driven her so far as to talk to the animals, to hear them as her only friends, left her.

Martina wanted to stop this girl she saw in the square and talk to her. But she knew the thoughts of that day: nothing was more important than that she go to the square with a purpose.

She was captured by the different way of living: the life those guys showed her, that unassailable feeling, the speeches, attitudes, music, and smiles. She had found a place among them, any time, day and night.

It was late at night on the prairie; only the clouds flowed with pulses like before.

Martina looked at them with uncertainty; she had lost the determination to look into her past and was almost tempted to follow Ginetta's advice and enjoy the possibilities of this no-memory place.

But sometimes in front of danger or disaster, there is a strange instinct to go inside, perhaps for the frenzy to get out as soon as possible, or the wish to catch a hope beyond the tragedy.

As following an unconscious desire, the clouds began to fall again, obscuring images of the prairie and the silence in which she was wrapped. The city appeared, and the square, on one of the many afternoons, she had sat on the edge of the fountain.

#

So she had met Daniel on the steps in front of the fountain, he and his guitar, his face turned down. He was all one with the music and didn't care about the people stopped to listen before taking the bus; he was seeking the best harmony, trying and trying.

When somebody asked for a song, he shook his head and smiled.

Martina, just arrived, was sitting in front. She had put her schoolbooks on the ground and was sitting on them. She put her head in her hands and swayed to the beat.

In one of the many breaks, she had met Daniel eyes. "Hello, my name is Martina—and yours?"

"Daniel!" He offered his name in a very short break.

"I've never seen you around here before; where are you coming from?" Martina asked insistently, interrupting the flow of the music.

Without answering, the boy stretched out his hand in the direction of one of the roads that converged on the square.

"How stupid you are!" she said, moving away with a disapproving look.

Daniel did not even raise his head or give her the chance to know if her curse was successful.

She saw Daniel the next day; her anger was gone.

Sometimes the stormy meetings had an unpredictable result, so the boy—short, thin, hair like a hedgehog and eyes unreachable—began to enter into Martina's thoughts.

She was sure about her Daniel's interest that time in a trip to the mountains. Every trip was an excuse to go in a quiet place to smoke and listen to the music in peace. Six of the town square group in two cars headed toward the woods on the mountain.

The cars were real scrap, and climbed the winding roads emitting noises like lamentations. In the car ahead, the party was started before they reached the woods. They had to stop twice on the plots next to the main road because one of the engines needed to take a break.

They arrived exactly at the hour programmed for the return. The sun was setting; they found some large stones and put them in a circle and lit the fire.

It was up to Martina and Daniel to search for firewood, and because of the speed with which the dry firewood burned, the trips to and from the woods were continuous.

Somewhere in an awkward place, their hands had met,

and, for a moment, they hesitated to bring them apart.

Martina asked herself many times why the touch of a hand at a awkward point had caused such a wave of heat. The time seemed to have stopped. Nothing was more important than that heated feeling: no trip, no friends— nothing else. Her heart seemed like it could burst. She had wanted to close her eyes, get into the heart to hold that happiness and loving moment.

Daniel later became her boyfriend, but in a way that she could never define. There was a sense of elusiveness around him like a halo. Many times she wondered if their love was true. She never had a definite answer.

#

Gianni arrived in the square near the same period as Martina. Often they spoke to each other, sitting on the edge of the fountain or in one of the four bars at the corners of the square.

Gianni always talked of moods and described his theories. Every problem for him he evaluated in very long discussions. Never had he refused to meet any difficulty, no matter where it came from or to whom it belonged.

Many people in the square could not live without his words of comfort. No one could be sad in the square without Gianni joining him and trying to make him smile. It seemed like a mission. Gianni was ready even to discuss with the fathers and mothers upset to see their children live in the middle of the square, so far from where they would want.

He did it not only to defend his friends. The worries from parents made him sad; he wanted them to understand and accept their sons' choices. Martina often espied his attitude: the way be behaved with others, his extraordinary sense of interest. So she thought that Gianni was a kind of comforting angel in the right place at the right time.

But sometimes, he was obsessive in his constant need to define, discuss, and comfort, to search at all costs for a plausible solution, and feel himself to be important.

Martina believed that sometimes the exhausting search for a reason or solution belittled the problem itself, reducing it to a kind of mathematical equation. Sometimes she felt that silent participation would had been more appropriate.

Then she felt an instinctive revulsion toward him and his attitude; she went away slowly without his noticing, her leaving, which would have another issue to be resolved.

However, when Gianni was missing from the square, they all needed somebody to talk to; no one was able to tame problems like he could.

It was really a bad day when Martina noticed something different about him. There were symptoms of the disease that was difficult to heal. She knew these symptoms well because she had learned how to defend herself.

Gianni fell into heroin, and how that happened deepened her hatred toward those people.

He had thought to help a friend to get out from it; he had entered into their group as the only way. Boldly he had faced the situation, convinced of his power and unaware of what reaction he might have.

Gianni was immediately surrounded by all the junkies; each one had a problem to define, a sentence to cry, or seemed touched by unhappiness and misfortune. Everybody had a sad story to tell and a lot of lost money.

Gianni offered words and money without caring in which of the two they would be most interested.

Martina did her best to take him away from those people; she took him aside, rebuking him and shouting her disapproval. She broke out in tears to try to change his mind.

"You're my best friend, you know! So you can't ask me not to help those who need me. If there is only one chance to get him out, I have to try! Don't worry; I don't run risks!" he whispered, and sadly smiled.

Martina and Gianni had a dream together, one of many between friends: to go far away, leaving the city.

"You'll see, when the time comes we'll go away—you and I alone around the world."

Gianni had a beautiful bike of which he was proud. Even Martina sometimes rode it up in the streets of the city. He had purchased it working as waiter for the whole summer. She was jealous of his bike.

In a short time, Gianni sold it, and all the guys around became great friends. He did not take a step without being followed, like a mother hen with her chicks. His followers would approve any speech or any theory, and, most important, that he pulled out money from his pocket.

In a short time he lost weight; his face took the appearance of an elderly person. His back began to bend, bringing his eyes more and more toward the ground.

His kingdom lasted the time of the bike's money; then no one came looking for him. He was like everyone else and began to crawl through the alleys, looking for his dose.

Night-time he could be seen leaning against the columns drowsy or asleep. Run away if somebody came up to talk to him. He looked frightened if touched on the shoulders, and he seemed in a terrible struggle against another world.

At any perceived presence, he fled like a drunken man, looking with his hands for a safer place. He dragged himself to the next wall, crawling to another hiding place.

One night Martina and Daniel found Gianni lying on a bench just off the square. Breathing heavily, he seemed to be asleep. They shook him vigorously, because he did not seem to show any other signs of life.

After having lifted him and put him in the car, they brought him home.

"Go away, I do not want to know anything," said his mother. "I bet it's your fault if he is in that condition. Go away; if not, I'll call the police!"

They spent the whole night trying not to fall asleep. They walked on either side of him for a long time, to keep him awake.

Dawn seemed to revive him; he broke free, and, without saying a word, he went away.

In the next days he spent his life between cheating and petty theft. He was captured by the police one night while he was stealing. He negotiated the sentence and was soon let back into a community.

He came back to the square a few months later; although he was a little aged, his eyes were lively again. He found a job; in the square, there was only in the evening. He told about the next future: who was going to live for a while in a village on the mountains with his uncle, who would give him a hand with the work on the hut, and would resume books to study.

His new prospect took not more than a month. He was surrounded again by his old friends and soon was one of them.

Sometime he would not be seen around, and then Martina hoped he was really up on the mountain.

Gianni was found in an overdose, lifeless in the bathroom of a bar in a town a few miles from his hometown. Nobody knew him there and it took a few days to find his family.

Martina cried for days; the memory came back to the good times they had spent together. The more she was thinking, the more the memories became beautiful and felt sad and alone. She thought what Gianni had done to all of them and how little they had done for him.

None of his friends was at the funeral.

#

The tears slid slowly from her eyes to her cheeks and so to the ground. Her eyes were open when the clouds lifted and the image of the prairie formed again.

She felt a terrible sadness; a helpless and lonely feeling was transformed into rhythmic sobs. She had not been sensitive enough about the problems of one of her greatest friends. She had not done enough to save him from the terrible disease.

With the memory she had found a friend, only to lose him again and feel the guilt.

Maybe sitting in the square and watching him die slowly mitigated a little the pain, but bringing back the memory and seeing it disappear forever made the situation sadder.

Her tears dried; her sobs subsided slowly.

She remained silent for a long time, watching intently the prairie. There were so different, the sensations up here...

#

Luisa arrived in the square in the fall. She was housed in a girls' boarding school; just off the square. She had been conducted there by a court order after she had been removed from the street and from the family confusion in a town not far away.

Her mother was a prostitute, and she grew up going from house to house, between uncles and neighbors.

At thirteen, she ran away, traveling along Italy until she was discovered in Piazza Maggiore in Bologna.

The first time she appeared, she was sitting around the fountain to listen to music from Daniel's guitar. Martina was sitting on the opposite side.

A huge amount of hair covered her face. She was a slender figure, with Mediterranean characteristics. Her eyes deep and black expressed a smile out of the ordinary, coming from her soul and her whole body; everything in her was involved in that smile.

When Martina saw that smile, she realized she had found a friend.

They spent whole evenings talking like two vessels that wish to exchange their contents. They walked the streets of the city as two sisters, always together.

Luisa said that when she reached eighteen, she was going away, far away from the people in the square. She did not like the city; people were not inclined to become familiar.

At reaching eighteen, she would have erased everything from her mind, leaving only a special space, jealously guarded for the friends in the square and especially for Martina.

Luisa had a great desire to live, believe in life, and, above all, believe in friends. Everybody were careful to give her no problems.

When taking someone's arm she held him so hard that it hurt; she seemed to want to hold that feeling, that friendship so precious.

Martina accompanied her almost every night in college, at a late hour, past the allowed curfew. Often, for punishment, they were prohibited to go out, but she never missed appointments and was able to escape through the window and reenter.

When they could convince Daniel, they went up in the mountains or lakes near the city. On those occasions, Luisa was happy: her face became radiant, her eyes were shining that like mirrors inside.

Luisa also really liked Daniel; Martina had noticed but did not feel hurt—her friend was the one who needed more affection. She imagined them together, and it did not feel so bad; she could bear it just to see her friend happy.

One time, late in the afternoon, Luisa came to the square crying. Her mother was arrived in the city. She had arrived with a lawyer and would soon be back for her. They had challenged the decision and were near to a judge rethinking.

Her mother had shown kindness and had promised a change of life, just to get Luisa back, she would find an honest job.

But Luisa was not going to come back with her.

One afternoon, her mother came to pick her up in the square and took her away in a very brutal manner.

The next day Luisa escaped from college; she asked for Daniel, because she needed a ride—she said to anywhere, but as far away as possible. She picked up her stuff and the little money she had saved. Her friends also made a collection.

When she got into the car, through the window, with tears in her eyes, she said, "Isn't it bad luck? Damned bad luck, to run away again? I just found some friends, and I have to go away!"

"Come on, don't complain!" said Martina. "You wanted to escape at eighteen! You anticipated just a little!" She smiled, opened the door, and stepped out to embrace Martina again.

"You'll see—I'll be back!" she said. "Soon, when everything will be quiet, I will still be here."

Daniel was said to have accompanied her to the Verona train station. For all the way, she had done nothing but cry. Daniel asked her several times if she was convinced about this decision.

"I have no alternative; if you knew what happens in my mother's home!"

Luisa wandered to Italy again, they could not find her.

Every week she phoned home to reassure all but didn't agree to return, given the circumstances.

It was three, maybe four months before she came back, months in which Martina had always wondered how she managed to survive. She had an uncommon art to not succumb.

Luisa returned to her previous conditions: she would never have gone to live again in her mother's house; but with her uncle, the only likeable family member, but only on the condition of being able to decide herself about the life and future choices.

Luisa came back in the square a year later; she arrived shining, like a soldier from a victorious war. At her side was a tall, blond boy, like a Prince Charming.

Her smile was shining even more, like Martina remembered.

She also had a little envy about this guy. She wondered if this guy knew how very lucky he had been, to be with a girl like Luisa.

#

Martina could not remember the exact moment when met Laura; after a while, she seemed to have known her for a very long time.

She had her first experiences with smoke together with Laura. When they could find a small piece, they ran away together and enjoyed, than came back to the square, laughing. Every situation, every person, seemed funny. The smoking effect in them was doubled.

Once they saved some money and decided to buy just a little. They would later sell to friends and then go to make a trip just together.

They had a safe address.

They went towards Bolzano, the designated place to make the purchase.

On the way back, after having smoked just a little for testing, they were overcome by panic, the fear of being stopped by police.

"And if we get caught? If there is a checkpoint by police ahead?"

They looked around, terrified, imagining a cop at every street corner.

Just before the town, there really was a checkpoint. There were two cars and six policeman with their guns drawn. Laura slowed down; Martina looked terrified.

"Stop; let's go back!" Laura said

"Do not be silly—go ahead! If not, they'll run after us!"

Laura came forward with the car slowly; the police were aware of the hesitation and alert.

The few seconds it took to get close to Martina seemed eternal; her heart was pouring.

When they were side by side, one of the officers approached the window and looked inside; he smiled and pointed for them to move on.

When they arrived in the square, they were still shaking.

Martina had knew that it was the end of career selling smoke; since they avoided even walking with a few pieces in his pocket.

Their friendship did not vanished when Laura began to attend political gatherings. She tried, unsuccessfully, to introduce Martina to such environments.

Laura could not endure the guys in the square, their inaction in the face of so many problems. She cursed them and their lack of backbone.

She went around the town with a spray can in pocket and, when darkness fell, could be seen as a ghost wandering among the few walls that were still clean.

One day she confided that when it was the revolution, she would be able to fight, even holding weapons.

In the few city protests, she was always at the head of the marches.

Their friendship had not reduced yet; Martina accepted her speeches and vision of a society of people all the same. She tried to understand but often could not. Sometimes, Laura realized that, when Martina said yes it was without understanding; then she would get very angry.

"But you did not understand anything then!"

Martina smiled and shrugged her shoulders.

But Laura was the only one to remember the birthdays and anniversaries—was the only one to come to the square, holding a flower on the day of Martina eighteenth birthday.

Laura comforted Luisa when she had to flee, ran straight home, took all her savings and gave it to Luisa with no regrets. She cried in a long rage when Gianni left them forever.

Laura and Martina's friendship did not fade even when they were summoned to the police station. That was the first time Martina met Sergeant Panebianco.

The police sergeant arrived in the square in the afternoon to announce the girl's call to the police station the next morning.

Martina came into the sergeant office's after Laura. She did not even have time to look into her friend face to find out what was the matter.

She was made to sit on a wooden chair in front of the desk sergeant. It was a small room consisting of a shelf by the window and two desks: one for the Sergeant, and a smaller one for the Corporal bent over an electric typewriter.

Old paintings with the heroic deeds of the Corps were hung on the walls.

The Sergeant spent a few minutes shuffling papers on his desk before speaking. Martina was terrified.

The young policeman occasionally raised his eyes watching her.

The Sergeant stopped writing on a sheet, raised his head, looked at Martina, pulled out a red folder, and opened it.

"Your name is—Martina!" He nodded with a smile. "Nineteen years. Profession…" He paused uncertainly; the profession did not appear in the paper in his folder.

"What is your profession?"

Martina was also uncertain about defining her profession.

"Student—but not too much; I dropped out of school for a while, and now I'm waiting."

"Yeah—waiting," snorted the Sergeant. He closed the folder and put it on top of a stack with other similar folders.

"Anyway, I am Sergeant Panebianco, commander of

this station; we called here to ask you a few questions!"

He stopped to look for a logical thread.

"We have received information about your involvement in illegal activity."

Martina stiffened in fear and immediately thought about the time they purchased the smoke. How had they found out? She cursed the unhealthy idea of obtaining some money in the sale.

"Mr. Sergeant, I have not done anything!"

The Sergeant smiled.

"Done nothing about what?" asked the Sergeant immediately.

Martina noticed the error; there was no need to rule out innocence even before being charged.

"I mean—I did not do anything—In general!"

The Sergeant smiled again; took off his glasses that had been resting precariously on his nose, and put them on the front desk.

"Miss Martina, you are nineteen. The same age as my daughter!" He brought his head closer to mean that the dialogue had become personal. "What are you doing all day like a desperate—" He paused, shaking his head. "In that square?"

This question she could not answer; to this question she would not have been able to respond even to herself.

"I see; you don't understand or don't want understand! I will be more clear. Somebody reported facts about you and your friend. You go around talking about revolution, writing on the walls. You say you are also ready to take weapons to overthrow the system. So you go around to instigate the people."

"For instigating?" asked Martina, who could not believe that was the reason for which they were convened.

She had to smile, glancing toward the young policeman sitting in the desk; as if to expect his denial.

"Miss Martina, try to understand: we're not talking about politics; we are so far from politics. Do you understood what I mean?"

Martina did not understand much about politics; it was illogical to feel accused of propaganda. She would have abolished politics and never made propaganda. The only time she had been forced to listen to the speeches of politics was with her friend Laura, and always it had been a tremendous effort to understand her speeches.

In a flash she understood the situation! It was because of Laura that she was here—because of her propaganda. They had called her because she was Laura's friend.

She summoned a little courage. "Really, Sergeant, I do not make politics," she said, smiling and shaking her head.

"Seems to me the opposite!"

"Yes, I know, it may seem so, but it is because of my friend; sometimes she talks a little strange!"

"That's right! This is subversion!"

"No! Although it may seem, I assure you otherwise. She does so because she is often angry, but she does it so... she can laugh!"

Sergeant Panebianco, serious and impassive until that moment, smiled at such a definition.

"Miss, these are not things to laugh about; subversion is anything but funny!"

"No, sergeant, not to laugh in the sense you understood. Laura, my friend, often speaks without realizing what she's saying. She would never do those things."

He looked at her doubtfully. The other policeman stopped writing and looked at her curiously.

"My friend is so because she is always angry, even with me—many times she's told me to fuck off—but, really, these are only words; when she gets quiet, she doesn't remember anything!"

The Sergeant retrieved his serious tone. "Miss—it is not easy to believe your words. Here are the facts: some of your friends are seriously investigated and made explicit reference to Laura's friend. They talked about meetings and deadlines to keep. These are not just jokes or angry expressions!"

"I don't know anything about these meetings, but I can imagine the phrases. I'm sure her intentions are nothing subversive!"

Sergeant Panebianco replaced his glasses, raised his head, looked at the young policeman, and pursed the lips.

"I've alerted; for now, there is nothing against you, nor against your friend, but you are under observation; don't find yourself in bad situations, because then you'll come back here! And not for a chat."

The talk was over; Martina was expected to get up, but the sergeant took off his glasses and bent his head closer, whispering, "Miss Martina, why go around like that? Do you have anything more interesting to do than getting into trouble?"

These last words, made a certain impression. He did not seem to speak as the sergeant, but more as father to his daughter. "You dropped out of school, and are going all day around the square. Do you have nothing to do, some interests?"

He brought his head even closer. "Is it really a life to live? Without interest, without prospects? If you want your life a bit so… as an artist, then do it, really! Now you are not doing anything, just wasting your time and getting into trouble! And then"—lowered his voice, giving the impression of a speech strictly confidential—"It is not good for you, all that stuff you smoke! Take this information: sooner or later the brain will irreparably ruin, with no opportunity to go back!"

He pulled his head back and looked at the young policeman, who had not changed expression. He got up and opened the door, calling out to Martina.

She had tears in her eyes when going out; she met Laura in the lobby. They did not exchange words for a good part of the way towards the town center.

"What did they say?" asked Laura, a bit worried.

"Nothing in particular! But you have to be careful; they are checking us out!"

The reproof seemed to have produced no results in Laura; she fell back to curses. But from then on she was careful about making speeches like those she had made before. During the demonstrations, she was far from the front row. About Martina no longer had problems with politics but saw sergeant Panebianco many times.

CHAPTER FIVE

Johnny came to the square in the spring and left a deep mark in Martina's life.

To capture her attention, was not his reflective and a little upset attitude typical of many guys into the square, but his young age, perhaps no more than twelve years.

He came alone to the square in the afternoon, and soon was sitting near the fountain without talking to anyone. He watched the people, when he occasionally raise his bent down head; life to him seemed be excessively heavy.

At dusk he got up and went away slowly.

Martina had been watching him for a long time, trying to find the reason why he was between them. She had no doubt about his attitude, which she recognized for having had it herself some years earlier. But from so young a boy, she would never have expected it.

She thought about the risks he could meet. The junkies would never have respect about his age; there were many ways in which they could use him.

When Martina came to speak with him, she was not at

all sure what would say. Johnny was sitting on the edge of the fountain with his head down almost between his legs—those skinny legs that seemed to barely to hold up the rest of his body. His hair was curly and wild. When he lifted the head she noticed the sad look, even sadder to be seen on a young boy's face.

"Hello, my name is Martina; am I bothering you?"

She had thought out these words the night before, which seemed the beginning of a fairy tale. Johnny suspiciously looked at her.

"I don't know…"

Martina uncertainly smiled. "You don't know if I'm disturbing you or what?"

"No! I don't know if I want to talk to you!" He put again his head down. Martina felt taken aback by such determination.

"I just wanted to talk, to know why a kid like you is all alone all the afternoons. Do you have nothing else to do? I don't know… go to school or play with your friends?"

He raised his head again to show a defiant, almost angry smile. "What do you care? I don't come to ask why you stay here all day in the square? I already have just one mom; I don't need someone else to break my balls here!"

Martina pulled back, struck by this reaction.

"Go spend your talk with someone else!"

She stood in disbelief; watching Johnny, she didn't know what to do. She wished to reply in kind, but instead stood up slowly away from the fountain. Johnny kept his head down, completely indifferent.

She hurt to think that she had been treated like a rag from the person for whom she wanted to do something good.

She felt her pride strongly wounded, and not for the refusal to talk, which she had anticipated, but for that so violent and unfriendly way. A simple no would be enough, and she would have gone!

A few weeks after that sad meeting, Johnny still was in

square; as she had expected, he had made the wrong friends. Junkies carried him around like a mascot. They needed him to muddy the waters; and make appearance of normality. When there was some petty theft in supermarkets to do, they sent him forward.

No one checked him.

When they had to share their doses, they no longer went into hiding. He had become their carrier.

Martina suffered at considering the evolution of the situation and for leaving so quickly the battle to save Jonny. If she had not listened to her pride, she would probably have been able to approach him and maybe distract him from those people.

One afternoon she crossed Johnny on a street. He was walking alone, hands in his pockets, and staring straight ahead.

Martina slowed down with the intention to speak to him again. But she would never have had the courage if it was not for Johnny stopping in front of her.

He watched her for a moment, then smiled.

"What did you say your name was?"

Martina did not interpret that smile in a positive manner; she thought he was laughing about their last meeting.

"My name is Martina." She smiled just a little. "But the next time you answer me like last time, I'll give you two slaps; is that clear?"

Her reaction was more violent as had planned and surprised even herself. Johnny stopped smiling, looked at her for a moment indecisively, and finally turned and walked away, increasing his walk until he was running.

For the second time she had been taken aback. "What fool I was!"

She could not understand this strange response. She had broken any dialogue possibility for the second time. For a second error she could not forgive herself; there was no way she could see him again.

But she was surprised when the next day in the square, she saw him standing in front of her. He had gotten up from the steps of the fountain especially to meet her.

"Are you not still angry?" Johnny asked.

"No! Not anymore." She smiled at being offered a third opportunity. "And you?"

"Neither am I! You know, I was not serious last time, and I understand that you were upset. It was my fault!"

They both smiled. Johnny sat beside her.

"Your name is Martina, right?"

The girl nodded. She looked at those deep eyes, trying to discover their secrets. Johnny realized and hid his face after becoming red.

"Why did you become red? You were not so shy that day you sent me to fuck off!"

He looked up. "There! I had had it with you, and I did not want to hear a sermon!"

"Were you so sure I was preparing a sermon?"

"Maybe it was not so?"

"Maybe yes, maybe not! You closed the conversation too soon to find out!"

"Come on! I know you would. All the old ones, when they find a boy like me, feel compelled to teach life." Johnny understood her intentions even before she put them into action.

"To see you so I could not blame them."

"Excuse me—what's wrong with me? Why does everybody have to say what I have to do? Some people look at me and shake their heads. I'm not going to tell them what they can and should do; why do they not leave me alone?"

He had risen talking loudly. "They are all the same! Their behaviors suck, and then they tell me what I should do, what's right and wrong. But who gives them the right to decide what is the right choice?"

Martina looked amused; this time she would not make the error of responding in kind.

"Probably because you are not yet old enough to make mistakes like them."

"There! There is always the age history; what does age mean? Errors don't have age—they are just mistakes!"

At least he was not entirely wrong. He was gifted with extraordinary wit, but was agitating, a bit, too. Somebody had already stopped to watch them.

"Oh—boy, be calm; don't panic. I did not take any notes on your way of life! Take it easy; I'm not used to so unfriendly characters."

Johnny also took a look at the people. "Sorry, but I don't have a problem with you. This is my way of speaking, I swear!"

"All right! Let's go for a ride; we're causing confusion here."

She took him by the arm. They walked onto a side street; for the first time, she felt like a mom. But what could she say to convince him of the wrong way, the bad end to which he was destined? All she had was basically the same phrases repeated constantly by her mother.

"Do you mind if I ask you a little of your life?" she asked shyly.

"It depends!"

"Depends on what?" Martina was trying a way to find some weaknesses.

"By why do you ask!"

"I'm asking because you made me curious."

"I made you curious?" He turned and smiled, surprised.

"Yes, I'm curious about you. I'd like to know why somebody so young is here!"

"There are many people here, but you're not curious about them!"

"What about? I know them all; some may be surprise me but not make me curious; it's different!"

"Yeah! Probably yes."

So he began to talk about his life. He ended speaking only after they had walked several times around the square and surrounding streets.

His mother in the evening worked in a restaurant, and in the daytime for a few hours she cleaned house for a wealthy family. He was tired repeating the schools, because, he said, they are useless.

His mother woke up late in the morning and was sure Johnny was at school. Instead he was already in the square with many friends.

During his story Martina had wondered what was the difference between them, except for their ages. She was terrified of this situation, especially when Johnny wanted to know about her—why she was in the square.

Martina told her story, mitigating the most difficult moments; in the end it seemed like a fairy tale: a story filled of many difficulties but with rounded corners. On Johnny it had the opposite effect than she expected. He followed her story with great interest, without missing a word.

"One day I will be like you," he exclaimed in the end.

She felt stupid and embarrassed for the blunder.

They walked silently for a few minutes. There was nothing else she could say in repair.

"Now that we're friends, can I confide why I wanted to know you?" Johnny asked, slowing the pace and watching her reaction.

"Of course, otherwise, why we are friends?"

"You know; of all the people in square, you're the cutest. You were the only one to offer a little friendship. You're just nice—I like you!"

Martina turned to look at him; she could not understand what he meant.

"I know, I'm a bit young and don't understand how to behave, but I want ask you…"

His gaze was bent forward; their pace quickened. Martina was terrified, imagining the result of his speech.

"I want ask you—will you be my girlfriend?"

Formulating the request, he was stuck looking up at

her.

Martina stopped walking; not knowing the answer to give, she wanted to run away. She was terrified and would never be able to handle such a situation: how to deal with a boy at his first crush.

Johnny felt her indecision and was waiting for an answer.

"You're not angry about my confession? Is it true?"

Martina showed her best smile.

"Why should I; yours is a wonderful feeling, but I—"

"Yes, I know! Are you telling me that you can't, I'm young, I—"Martina interrupted him, taking his hand, she squeezed it between hers. "That's not the point, Johnny! I do not feel the same way. If two do not to get the same feelings, it makes no sense and can't work—you understand?"

"No."

"No matter your age, probably yours is a true feeling, but it is not shared by me! See, sometimes it happen to me the same for a guy, but I have to pretend nothing happened, because for him it is not the same thing."

Martina's look seemed implore Johnny, because he understood her point of view.

"I appreciate your sincerity, but I can't be your girl!"

The boy's face was sad; to him, hers was an incomprehensible position. They talked so much together, and she had agreed to spend the afternoon with him!

"You could try; maybe you'd be happy after!"

Martina was shaking, confused, her eyes shining. "Maybe, but I can't be your girlfriend, thinking only of a probability! It would not be honest to me and to you. It's better we remain friends, and then we'll see!"

The last sentence sounded terrible to Martina herself; she had always hated the phrase *remain friends*, as if the friendship was a surplus, a sop to the lack of love.

Many times she had had to defend against a sentence

like that. Now she was in terrible need to express that concept.

Johnny bowed his head, pulled the hand away from Martina, spun around and ran away.

"What a disaster! What a disaster!" she thought, walking on the opposite side.

"I did just a disaster!"

This time there was no prospect of repair, she would never again have the courage to approach him.

#

The days after Johnny avoided meeting Martina's gaze, he went out with new friends.

One afternoon, he unexpectedly came to sit beside her. His face was smiling a strange smile: mocking, challenging. A little surprised, she turned to watch him. The look stopped at the eyes—a too-familiar expression.

Immediately realized what had happened. She took his arm and with horror saw a red spot; he probably had had trouble finding the vein.

"Are you crazy! What have you done?"

Martina had risen, placing herself before him. Johnny smiled, enjoying the rematch.

"If you don't want to be with me, I don't care anymore! It's all your fault!"

Martina threw down his arm. Johnny stopped to look at her and bowed his head forward.

Frightened, she ran away, turning around the corner just as the tears came. The punishment inflicted was too hard. She could not bear responsibility for a boy adrift. Of course she had made mistakes, but she could not be punished so harshly. The blackmail was too heavy for an unrequited love, an evil only possible in a child's cold mind.

Martina walked all the afternoon through the streets of downtown; she went to hide behind a corner every time she felt the tears come. She could not find a solution. Toward evening, she found a possible way out.

#

Sergeant Panebianco recognized her immediately when he came to open the door of the police station. He was a little surprised and asked if anything had happened.

She felt anguish at seeing him sitting in that chair again. But the choice to turn to the Sergeant seemed it the best solution. He was the only one who could do something. Maybe that's the reason why she was surprised when, at the end of her story, the Sergeant asked, "What do you think would be the best solution, Miss Martina?" The Sergeant was asking her advice.

"Actually, if you don't know, you… Sergeant… I think he should be removed from the square, but I don't know how!"

"It is not so easy, you know! I was not able even to remove you from that square." He looked at her, smiling; Martina became red with shame.

"I could bring him here, give him a lecture, maybe hold him few hours to scare him, but I know how it ends: tomorrow he would still be in the square with his new hero image in front of the others, and the result would be much worse than the cure!"

Martina had never seen the problem from that point of view.

"I, Sergeant… I would not know what to do!"

"Yeah, how do?" He paused, then went ahead to say, "We could do it this way: first of all, we will make our presence known, in a discreet way, without taking him away; at the same time, we find his mother. I will go myself to talk to her."

"I think it's a good solution!"

Martina was very worried; the Sergeant smiled. Looking at her, he felt the tragedy of the situation and wouldn't ever have expected a collaboration from her. He rose to accompany her.

"Well, Miss Martina! We'll talk to you later, then!"

"Yes, Sergeant, good-bye!"

When Martina was at the door, she turned to look at him again; did not feel completely satisfied. The Sergeant seemed to have waiting for that response and smiled again.

"Miss—are you doing the right thing, you want to know. Don't worry; we will solve the problem."

"I hope so!"

When she walked through the door she felt fine, sure that she had done the right thing. She returned to the square, waiting; Johnny was always surrounded by junkies. He occasionally passed in front of her and smiled. Sometime he sat nearby with dazed face. Martina braced herself against her desire to run away.

A few days later, on the way home, a police car crossed in front of her. On board was the Sergeant Panebianco; he rolled down the window. "Miss, we were looking for you. I spoke with the Johnny's mother, who would like to see you. The meeting is for tomorrow morning at the police station!"

The day after she was again in that office, sitting in the chair that had become so familiar. The Sergeant recommended she be calm, no matter what happened. The mother, he suggested, might not have take it so well. The second chair next to Martina was to indicate that Johnny's mother would come soon.

Five minutes later arrived a woman about forty, with matted hair and Johnny's same dark eyes, came up, gesturing toward Martina. "It's her, Sergeant? She was telling you about my son? Said that my son is a junkie? Seems to me she is junkie; how do you believe her?"

The Sergeant replied, rising from his chair, "Sit down, lady! Sit down, and don't say bad things. In these two days, we checked out in the square, and it is absolutely true!"

Martina was going to cry, her eyes could barely restrain

against the impulse. The Sergeant understood the situation and turned back to the mother: "Ma'am, there's a problem to deal with and we have to face it together. You'll have to give up any kind of hesitation toward this young woman!"

The mother still could not see Martina's face; only, with quick glances sideways, she tried to assess her.

"I don't want any fuss about the way of life of Miss Martina and neither should you criticize decisions about your son's education. I just want to say that the problem exists, and should be addressed without delay, now!" he looked at the mother and then Martina—"And when I say *now*, I mean that could also be later today. The only possibility is to intervene immediately and carry him away from the square."

Martina nodded and turned slowly towards the mother; the woman was still stiff.

The Sergeant continued to speak directly to the mother. "If you really want to save Johnny, you must put by any resentment and think only of his own good. Most of all, you needs Miss Martina's help to save your son. No one better knows the situation, and it is necessary to take advantage of your son's love for her. For this reason, you must find together, maybe with my help, a way to work together."

The mother bowed her head for a few minutes and wept slowly. Then she looked at the Sergeant and finally to Martina.

"I'm sorry if I hurt you, but this situation makes me so upset…"

Martina smiled reassuringly. The woman smiled back. "My name is Sandra!"

The Sergeant took a deep sigh of relief.

#

The two women left the police station and walked slowly to the square. Sandra asked her to help her see her son in secret. They hid behind a corner near the square, where the streets turn at right angles.

Johnny was walking a few steps away, together with three well-known junkies, looking around surreptitiously like they were. Sandra could not hold back the tears. Martina restrained the woman's instinct to run to her son, by holding on to her and then leading her away.

They spent the rest of the morning together at Sandra's home around the kitchen table.

It was a small, rented apartment just outside the historic center. Two rooms and a balcony, adorned with geraniums. The kitchen was bare and a naphthalene smell came from the other rooms.

The woman's face was furrowed by deep wrinkles and her body was dried; her figure was lost, to prove that beauty passes too quickly. After separation from her husband, she had worked as a waitress in the bar, following impossible schedules.

She wanted to know about Johnny, how he had fallen into drugs so soon. She listened attentively, sometimes interrupting Martina to better understand the terminology. Sometimes she passed a handkerchief over her face stopping the continuous tears from streaming down.

She wanted to know about Johnny's infatuation with her. She smiled, looking at the girl and trying to figure out where a child's love was born. She shook her head at such a feeling at so young an age. Martina also had some crying; she felt some responsibility belonged to her.

For three days Martina spent the afternoons with Sandra, talking of Johnny and studying strategies. Over the past two days, Johnny had not back home. They must act quickly.

At last day of the week at Sandra's home came the Sergeant; he was not wearing a uniform, which to Martina seemed odd. Sergeant guessed her thoughts and smiled, not at all offended.

All was set for the next day; they were going to take

him from the square to the police station. In the evening, Sandra would go to the station to take him with his bags already loaded into the car, to go away, far away from the city. In Verona, there was his brother waiting for them.

As evening greeted Sandra, she hadn't the courage to return to the square. She went home, gripped by pain.

The next day happened as had been planned; Martina did not go to the square but turned along the streets of the suburbs instead. She did not want to attend when they loaded him into the car. Sandra was also timely. She took his son to the car in tears.

Johnny disappeared forever from the square; in a short time, the apartment in which he and his mother had lived was occupied by another person.

#

Martina, after a month, returning home, she found her mother at the door waiting for her; it had been Sergeant who had asked for her. He had left a letter from Sandra.

Dear Martina,

I need to write! I apologize if I still am taking advantage of your time. It's almost night now, and Johnny is sleeping. Today we had a busy day: I went to school to talk with the professor and discussed the problem. He was understanding and told me he'll take care of the problem.

Here we are fine; we found a small apartment and I started, as you suggested, talking to Johnny. It was not so difficult. At the start he did not want to, but then let go.

Today was also my first working day. I'm here in a bar with so many guys. Who knows, maybe I'll learn something too. Probably this place is not different from yours, and where lived—also my Johnny.

I don't know if this is a mistake, but when I look at these guys, I see a bit of you, and I feel sadness. Surely there may be somebody among them with the same problems as Johnny, and for each of them there is a mother like me, suffering.

But I was lucky; my lucky was meet you!

I know, you also have big problems, and only now I realize that I have been selfish. While you were giving us your help, I did not think to talk about your problems.

How do I fix my mistakes and give you a hand! I'm sorry, and I pray that somebody can at least be nice to you as much as you've been with us.

If it's any consolation, you need to know: between us, there is always a part of you.

Often in the evening, Johnny and I talk a lot about you. We say you're a great girl. You know, he is still very much in love, and I don't feel he's going to finish too early this first adult dream. When, in the future, he'll find a girl, I hope she looks like you, and has the same sensitivity.

This is not the first letter addressed to you, but they are all still here. I had not the strength to send the letters before, and I don't know if I can send this.

I just want reach you with a bit of peace that I am feeling now; that is my best wish for you. When I feel strong enough, we'll come visit you; Johnny's asking me every time. Who knows, maybe when you least expect you will see coming.

I would like you to come a bit of my friendship with this letter.

Hello soon, a kiss and a hug!

Your Sandra, with love.

#

Crying, Martina read and reread the letter many times.

After a few months, they were in town to visit her. They arrived in the square around noon and took off all day until sunset.

Johnny hugged her so tightly he forced Sandra to tear him away. He was so excited to look at her, he was not able to speak; but when he finally relaxed, nobody could shut him up.

It was a different Johnny in front of her—far from that boy in the square. His eyes had become lively. Sandra, she also was different. They walked the streets hand in hand.

After this visit, Martina did not see them again. Sandra stayed in contact with Martina, telling of Johnny, until his love for her vanished.

Then she did not hear of them anymore.

#

For many years, Martina spent the days among the four streets around the center. She was a square resident all hours, till late in the evening.

Everything seemed to flow normally, behaving in the same way, but after Johnny's story, something had changed. She felt strong feelings and thought long about this. Fear, anger, helplessness and affection: a bit of everything remained fixed in her.

Her mind was loaded with a new strength: a spirituality impossible to define. Sometimes it was hard enough to cancel any other thought. She closed her eyes, and imagination took her over.

Sometimes, when she stood together with the others listening to music or in silence, something strange happened in her, as if her mind would take her away. Then the square, friends, nothing existed except those strange thoughts.

Martina had a diagnosis: the cause was the result of many smokes to have produced an abnormal reaction of her mind. It was enough just for the sun to produced strange shadows on the walls because her mind was taken away by the strange effects and began to fantasize.

Any weather event, a cloud a bit strange, a colorful sunset, but also the strange passerby's face, an old car's creaking, the music coming from an open window—any of these could take her away. Everything seemed to attract her and her wandering thoughts as powdered iron to a magnet.

Her perception changed and magnified, and she looked the other people as if she could understand their thoughts, read their moods, and guess their intentions.

It was so intense that introspection would always take her away. Even if her friends went away and other people came and sat beside, she did not realize it.

No one gave much attention to Martina's new attitudes; such behavior was understandable after smoking. But this intense mental activity was not related to the moments of smoking; on the contrary, it was more pronounced when the mind was free.

The development of her imagination was powerful, but weak and delicate like a light breeze at the same time—it was difficult to understand. What her mind undertook was not deep meditation or analysis; rather, something more gentle, to be seized without any programming, a charge inside, a heat throughout her body, a strange desire to gather herself in and close her eyes.

Which was enough of a violent thought to chase away her imagination, which would all vanish without a chance to resume.

Once she wanted to enter the church on the square. She had always hated the big doors opening on Sunday morning, the people flowing back and forth, all together. They had passed by her smiling with contempt.

But once she decided to enter, on a hot summer afternoon when no one walk around the square.

She slowly opened the door. The contrast with the strong external light gave the impression of entering another world. She walked slowly, coming to sit on a bench in the back of the church.

There was an odd smell and an eerie silence. The big signs and sometimes bloody images reminded her of Sunday mornings, when she was still a child. The fearful images of martyrs' violent deaths were painted on the walls.

Religious functions had always given her the impression of a collective game, a series of questions and answers between who stood up at the altar and the people down below. Whoever guessed correctly went to the altar to receive the award; a small white particle. She always fell asleep during functions and would not have ever gotten the award.

There were also the songs and the incense smell.

She closed her eyes and a smile followed other memories as other images took shape: the Sunday morning, the old farmhouse where she had lived her early years, porches, and a large yard where the cows, carrying calves, went out to pasture.

In the air there was the countryside smell that the farmers brought into the church, the intense and pungent manure's smell was mixed with the incense scent.

Her thoughts began to run fast till they would stop at something strange. She saw the sky, a great and boundless blue sky crossed by white clouds that walked like sheep back to the fold. She saw a willow tree in the countryside, and she saw herself as she stood leaning against the trunk to look at the sky.

She was taken away: disappeared was the church, the darkness, the pictures on the walls. She could see only the clouds floating—nothing else than that inscrutable, slow flow. Even breathing seemed to have stopped in a long and great pause.

She did not realize the time spent in contemplation, when she was hit on the shoulder.

"Miss, need anything?" A face as dark as his cassock was leaning toward her and waiting for an answer.

Martina, suddenly roused from her trance, jumped.

"No, no thank you!"

"All right!" said the old priest, waiting a bit before leaving.

Her heart was beating fast, having been torn brutally from the dream.

She waited a moment to compose herself, then slipped off the bench and walked slowly away and back outside.

In the square she sat around the fountain, uncertain of her presence there.

CHAPTER SIX

Martina closed her eyes, and stood up, leaving the rock on which she was sitting. She walked slowly on dry land, around the bushes withered from waterlessness

The clouds were flowing with an intense pulse; they were calling her to continue to follow them. But she was worried, and her thoughts wandered carefully avoiding their calls. A strange uneasiness suddenly took hold of her. Her unease was not because of the dark, or even the wind's noise in the dry bushes or the woods themselves far to the plateau. It was not because of her impression, in solitude of a place impossible to define.

It was inside her; she felt it without a reason given. In that square happened something to change her life; something important, whose effect had gone beyond the time when it had happened, like a bright light that projects its aura far.

A shiver ran down her back; she could not give up right now, she felt so close to the truth.

The clouds went ahead to call her, with intense light, to play again.

Martina hesitated; she could wait until tomorrow or even longer to discover the truth. She could ignore the truth's call and think about something else. She could go to sleep and put off until tomorrow any decision.

But would not be able to sleep, and every minute would filled with that feeling.

She slowly got back on her feet, and walked to sit on the same rock as before, and she waited.

The clouds wrapped around her again. The memories, before being displayed, proposed strange sensations, like the strange taste that every thunderstorms bring before: the scent of the storm.

#

Martina had just come out from the church, still immersed in the mystical flavor she had felt on the old wooden bench. There were many thoughts and images suddenly got into her head.

They started with childhood memories. What was left of her young age: the intuition, the long dialogues with animals? Where was gone the imagination that had been able to understand their emotions, to feel the change of seasons, to be apprehensive if some clouds hid the sun for too long?

All was over, in the next years she had even felt ashamed.

Leaving the church, she had found the old thoughts; she did not know why, but, as if by magic, they were back in her head, and she was able to remember the past and what she had lost.

Maybe it was the last pulse of the lost childhood, or a warning about her life. Walking through the streets of downtown, the strange spirituality stood there in front of her, like a mirror reflecting another person, so alike but different. So present but impossible to grasp. Like a memory, a dream could be felt with the precise fidelity of its flavor, but it dissolved if she tried to grab it.

If it did not took much guesswork in her mind and she has not haunted by doubts, the fantasy would come and touch her mind. So the orange bus, having just turned the corner, became a large, rocking boat on the river. She read the thoughts of an old dog crossing his path, so she followed him, curious, trying to ask where he came from, where he was going, and if he was sad or happy.

Even a pigeon on the pavement of the square—it was like an old silent-film star. Martina laughed for a long time, watching his scampering disconnected.

But then she got back to herself. "But what am I doing? I must have smoked too much; I can't take control of my thoughts."

Even the atmosphere around the square that afternoon seemed to be part of the oddities. There had been a rabid sun, until threatening blacks clouds covered the square, leaning on the higher roofs. For a long time they were about to unleash thunder and lightning, but then the sun was back. When no one would have expected, it had returned, more menacing than before. At the end, a strong wind had swept everything away, like an authoritarian hand had interrupted the strange game of the two contenders.

After a long walk, Martina was sitting on the edge of the fountain. The other inhabitants of the square had arrived. They spoke to each other, laughing and joking as usual.

That evening, within her head, Martina could not be among them. She was walking in the air, staring, away from everyone else. Even when they came to tell her that somebody had found a good piece of smoke and everyone would go to a nearby park to make a party, she followed them without realizing where she was going. She smiled at their words that she could not even hear; their talk was like so many strange noises come by accident into her head.

The joint ritual was performed, the same as many other times. Somebody asked if she was okay or had problems.

Martina, with a smile, gave an answer without understanding its meaning.

When the joint arrived in her hands, she inhaled and passed it, as was the custom. It made a second and a third round. It was now on another round, and more puffs rose from the center of the bench. The guitar changed hands, continuing to issue the same lamentations.

Martina was sitting at the side of the bench with her head down supported by her hands while her elbows rested on her knees.

Suddenly, her thoughts were freed from all heaviness. It was an unexpected sensation; her eyes closed in pleasure and her lips lifted in a smile. Clouds reappeared in the sky and without haste slowly flowed across an alpine landscape. She followed their movements as if she was a part of them.

Soft hills with grass like a green carpet alternated between their clouds, that were bouncing against them like tennis balls. She stood leaning with her back against the willow tree.

Martina saw white clouds in the sky of a blue hard to imagine in its intensity. A kind of earthly paradise where her thoughts finally could run free without any restrictions, where no distraction could detract from her search for the truth.

Everything was given over to complete the peace in her heart, the wind itself, and the scent of mountain meadows.

She wanted to get up, leave the dark park to get to her imagination, to discover up close and touch the grass, the clouds, the sky.

But despite every effort, she was always glued to the ground. There seemed to be strong arms to block her from running away. The bench on which she was sitting was not only a bench, but a huge weight she would never be able to get rid of.

The thought suddenly became sad, plucked from a sense of heaviness and helplessness; she opened her eyes and shook her head.

"I can't, I can't" she said with a soft voice, suddenly her mind went back next to the bench in the park.

"Don't do it!"

Instead of the mountain's vision, she was taken with a terrible sadness; she restrained the impulse to cry.

The sky and clouds were gone; there was only a sad and dark park on the outskirts of the city. Even her friends had gone away and had not even noticed her. Nobody had bothered to warn her. She was alone together with a failed dream and a terrible sadness. The thoughts had become heavy as a rock, seeming to want to take revenge for the missed opportunity.

Maybe if she had been in the square, perhaps under the lights, with the people around her, she could have thought differently.

Here, however, there was no one able to explain or get her some help; sadness made the park feel like a prison. All afternoon she had fed on illusions; now had to pay the piper. She was no longer a child and could not behave as such; she should have noticed before now.

Her thoughts had changed in a hurry; it were useless to grope for the images to drive away her sense of desolation by closing her eyes, in the hope that the dream could build better in the dark.

Instead, her fear became an image in which no eye could be closed.

"Leave me alone!" she yelled, clenching her head in hands.

She saw strange objects move around her: shadows and light reflections impossible to locate. The light from the car headlights hit her in the face and jerked her upright. She had the feeling that someone was hiding somewhere ready to assail her. Lights and shadows seemed to appear and disappear immediately.

She wanted to get up and run away, leaving behind those awful feelings, but she was not sure about being able to reach the road to run away.

Sometimes when her mind became clear, she realized the absurdity of these fears—it was just a dog complaining or sounds of car engines winding down or accelerate and turning, or the trembling leaves blown by the wind that made her fall back in fear.

She felt something strange in her throat: the terror seemed to materialize and condensed in a stream of oily fluid. Any attempt to swallow, the spit slid up the substance in her throat, making her jerk. She took some coughs to throw it outside, but it seemed stuck.

She felt a chill.

"Oh my god! It's inside me!'

#

She stood motionless, not knowing what to do. She had heard from older friends about a sort of rocking backward and the sudden terror that sometimes assails those who use hallucinogens. It's a paranoia difficult to escape. They said it was a kind of door which when opened, nobody is able to close.

Many people never came back from this trip.

They had talked about such a situation and recommended being near somebody to talk to, somebody stronger to hold on to, to be able to get back to normal feeling. But there was no one beside her; she was alone!

Furthermore, she had nothing to do with hallucinogenic substances! Nothing except the smoke! She had never used them, she's always had a fear of all those chemical things. But that substance that rolled up in her throat seemed to have those characteristics.

She decided to get up for a moment, and she seemed to be back normal, just in time to take a deep breath before feeling again the dizziness and roiling in her stomach that made her feel like vomiting.

She gone around the bench, then again. She turned by a

tree and ran, almost up to the road. The cars passed near her, slowing down, taking the curve and going away.

How could she be back in the square in this condition? She wondered what everyone would think of her. She had no intention to look like a junkie for the rest of her life. She would have to wait until the end of the hallucinations.

She sat back seat, wrapped her head in her arms, closed her eyes, and waited.

A sudden vertigo make her open her eyes again. She fell over to lay on the bench. Her stomach hurt; she felt she would vomit at any moment. her mouth was full of that strange substance; her heart was running fast, as if it was struck by fireworks. The strange oily substance climbed up her throat into her head and burst, emitting strong beams like lightning.

"My God, what's happening to me? am I dying? I Can't! I don't want to die!"

Her heart beat sharply; her eyes reported only terror.

She did not know how much time had passed; the last memory of the park was its dark, and a desperate dog barking. It came from far away and approached until she should feel it in her head. The dog barked so loudly it covered the noise of the cars in the street; she stretched out her hand to touch him, but there was no one nearby, just a bark, desperate as she was.

She was lifted, then felt a slight pain in her arm. She woke up on the ambulance couch.

\#

Having regained consciousness, she heard some people in white gowns talking to each other.

"Take her that way and lay her on the table. That's right—open the door; you can go now to the driver's seat and turn on the siren."

Before the ambulance doors closed, she had time to see some people who were watching her, talking to each other and shaking their heads.

"It's okay, girl, soon you'll be in the hospital. You'll be all right." The nurse tried to reassure her.

"Now, I should know about the drug so I can warn the emergency room."

"What do you think I took? It was only a couple of joints, nothing else!"

"Of course, a couple of joints" said the nurse smiling. "You were not reduced in this state by a couple of joints! However, if you don't want to tell me about the substance you took, it's all the same to me; it's your problem!"

Martina could feel her head burst and her heart breaking. She had no intention of retorting.

Before the ambulance started, she searched among the people for the dog with that desperate barking; maybe the dog was the one to rush people. There was no dog there, he had already gone.

The ambulance arrived at the hospital with sirens lit. They placed Martina on a small bed

"What's your name, girl?" asked the doctor; who had taken her into a room with white walls and gray polished metal. Next to him was a nurse maneuvering a strange machine. Martina had some wires attached to the head.

"Martina!" she said.

"Listen, Martina, which drugs did you take?" asked the doctor without any hesitation; his look was directed to the machine and its display of lines going up and down.

"I did not take anything strange; just a few joints."

"You have to tell the truth!" said the doctor, his gaze serious. "We want to help, but you have to tell the truth."

For a moment he looked away and pointed to the screen to his assistant:"You see? Rise… Rise… Rise… and then it falls all at once!"

The object of their speeches, Martina could feel the rise and fall in her head, those strange bursts of light.

"Listen, daughter," said the doctor, "I can well imagine what you've got; I don't even want to say"—his gaze was stern—"but I want to warn you of the risk involved; if it were not for a dog's insistent barking that attracted people in the park, you would not be here on this bed, but in another room down below, waiting for your funeral. Your heart would not hold."

A shiver ran down her back.

They gave her an injection and, immediately she began to feel relieved. The flashes degreases; her head stopped hurting.

She began to breathe normally, wiped her eyes, and looked around. She was in a small lit room; the hallway beyond the door was dark and silent.

Much better, she looked at the two doctors. She was able also to smile.

"Welcome among us!" said the nurse.

"I was really bad!"

"Yeah, but don't think about that now. You have a good sleep; then we'll see tomorrow."

Martina lost consciousness very soon, but not before feeling regret at not being anywhere else—in any other situation than this.

#

When she opened her eyes, the room was full of light; and a fly was buzzing on her nose. She did not realize immediately that she was in a hospital room. When she realized, it was terrible.

"Martina!" She heard whispering.

"Martina! How are you, dear child?"

She again closed her eyes as she felt the mother's presence; the thought of having to face her gave Martina anguish.

"Martina! What happened to you?"

She turned her eyes toward her mother; why had reality reopened with a big problem to deal with?

"Mom! I don't... I don't know!"

She took her mother's hand as her head filled with pain and her eyes with tears; she was looking for a logical explanation. "Mom, what are you doing here?"

"How… what are you doing here? They called, and I came here." She patted her daughter's head. "What happened to you? Tell me they are wrong—it can't be true! I know, sometimes you're a bit strange, but I can't imagine there's more, please!"

She began to cry.

"Mom! Not here, please!"

"Then it's true! You take drugs!"

For such question, on other occasions, would have made Martina smile. But here it seemed to be a process in which it was impossible to prove her innocence.

"It is not so! Whatever they have said is not true. I really don't know what happened to me last night!"

Her mother shook her head and covered her eyes with her hands.

"It did not happen last night, but the other day—you slept all this time!"

#

Martina slept another day and another night. She woke up with a fever and a terrible heaviness in her head and stomach.

She was able to eat, but the thoughts kept coming back to that night: nightmares and hallucinations. She could not give an explanation. In all the time she spent in the square she had kept well away from the hallucinogenic substances like LSD or Crack, normally used in the square, in order to avoid similar problems. She had learned to fight the normal depression and hunger after a massive smoke. But here it was something else, something bigger, and she could not figure out what it was.

The reason must be in that strange imagination, the fantasy started in the church and continued throughout the day.

It had been a powerful unknown force, much stronger than her will, impossible to resist. She had mistaken it for a positive force.

Martina thought back to that night, starting in the afternoon, and retraced each moment in hopes of finding a reference.

The room was full of light; it was warm. The sun beat against the glass of the large windows, breaking up into many small beams. A heavy curtain swung, driven by gusts of wind coming from an open window.

At some time a figure dressed in white opened the door and pushed a head inside to check on Martina. Someone smiled.

Martina felt suspicion in the eyes of the doctors, nurses and attendants; she felt that they had cast her in a role that she did not belong in, as a defendant wrongfully convicted. But she had declined to provide explanations, so perhaps, in their position, she would have thought the same way. She just wanted to be sent away—to get away from there and forget all the nightmares.

In the afternoon Sergeant Panebianco came to see her. He took off his hat upon entering the room. His face was sad and silent. Before leaving, he asked her to go to the police station, as soon as she was discharged.

Her mother, and Daniel, the only one of her friends, came to visit in the afternoon.

Finally, the next day, came the time to leave the hospital, after the doctors visited her for the last time and warned of the risks she was going to meet.

Martina did not call anyone to pick her up; she wanted to make the way back by foot, alone.

She crossed the hospital door, took a deep breath, and looked up at the sky. Some white clouds floated slowly, immediately captured her attention, such as sweet music from which there is no escape.

Martina smiled, following their call but was immediately

seized with fear; the last time she had followed the clouds, she had ended right in the place she had just left.

Brought back immediately, she looked down and walked without thinking about those clouds.

#

Facing the meeting with Sergeant Panebianco was difficult; she put it off for a few days, but finally had to go.

"Sit down!"

His voice and eyes seemed distant. A long silence followed his listening to Martina's story.

"I not telling you that I don't believe; I'm used to strange things. Sometimes I pretend to believe, and sometimes I really believe. But what sense does your story make, Miss Martina?"

He seemed to beg. "What sense does it make to be in the midst of such experiences? What sense does it make to take those substances whose effect is not clear, light or heavy as they are? What did you want to prove to yourself? To be good, to be strong? Tell me, what did you want to prove?"

"I don't know!" Martina was confused. "I don't know!"

Everyone says 'I don't know,' then after are immersed in the biggest problems! I don't know what was the reason to end it in the hospital dying, but motivation is not important, and the answer is always the same: it was not worth it! You risked really big."

His expression was hard and stern; Martina could feel the weight. She could hardly hold back the tears.

Sergeant Panebianco noticed. "Miss Martina why did you let it go? What sense is there to play with life in this way? Why throw away that good feeling, so rare to find in people? You had no right to throw away your life like that. You have your whole life ahead, all the possibilities open, you can do whatever you wants—why risk ending up dead?"

Martina lowered her head and did not know what to say; she no longer had the strength to try to clear herself. Neither did the Sergeant know what to add up or how.

"You can go now!" He said, standing up.

"Can I go?" She was surprised; she had been expected some questioning about the substance taken and who had made it available.

"Of course, you can go; I've not brought you here to find out what I already know!"

She had such confusion when she left the police station, she didn't feel like going back home and even to the square. She instead walked on the streets of downtown, avoiding the park where she had suffered so much.

She understood the meaning of the Sergeant's reproaches, but they did not quite fit; the reason was behind the smoke of that night.

She stopped behind a corner surrounded by sadness; she might as well become a junkie—all the evidence was against her.

#

The next day Martina avoided going to the square, a bit out of shame, a little because she didn't feel ready for what had become her normal life there. Something had changed; she had to wait.

Having taken a long walk through the city, she then took the road to the periphery. It was the same path she had taken every day, from the old house where she spent her childhood to where she had gone to town for school.

In a few years, the old country road had changed. There were no longer the stepping stones, the only to pop out when the snow covered the road. Instead of the ditch was a sidewalk and a bike path.

From the time she woke up in the hospital, not a moment had passed without her thoughts going back to the bad evening moments of the park.

"It must be some kind of disease! It never happened before, to suffer from nightmares so devastating!"

She sat on a bench on the right side of the road, next to the bike path, an imperfect strip at the edge of the roadway. A long row of trees lined the route. The wind seemed to enjoy the leaves and making them swing; the sunbeams rhythmically hit her in the face like an old transmission in Morse code.

All morning she had thought long and hard. Now she was tired; she wished she had already spent enough time to forget, like any sad situation that the memory can, over time, invert the negative impression. She was not asking for so much—just a bit of peace to soften the thoughts.

Martina gave a long sigh, moved to the end of the bench to avoid the pushy sun, relaxed her muscles, and bent her head back. The wind had made a deep blue sky; the few clouds threatening the blue were moving slowly. Her eyes immediately caught those clouds. The thought of clouds seemed to became an obsession.

Her attention was stolen from a bike approaching—an old, rusty bicycle. Every pedal stroke emitted strange noises, like pain twinges.

Following the sound, without raising her head, it seemed to Martina like crying. For every groan, Martina twisted the face and felt the pain getting inside her thoughts.

She wanted to console the pain—maybe it was because of old age—so she stretched out her hand as if to give a caress. The bike stopped a little further on; one foot touched the ground and a cyclist's surprised face turned toward her.

Martina pulled herself together.

Just as the cyclist passed, Martina put her head in her hands. "I'm going crazy! For sure, I'm getting crazy!"

She drew a long breath and leaned her head back. The sun was hot, but the wind flowed, slowly refreshing her face. The wind wore flavors of a country very far from there, wake up dormant memories. Particularly one seemed to prevail; it was the grass smell before the storm, when the wind prepares to welcome the rain. The grass bent under its thrust, shaking off the dust.

A distant thunder made real this impression. Fat clouds floated in the sky, preparing to come forward.

She closed her eyes, savoring the scent, but there were other clouds in her thoughts, more agile and soft. The difference between the two was the same as between a sound and a melody, a photograph and a painting.

Closing her eyes, she saw the clouds of imagination appear next to her thoughts, together with a sense of well-being and tranquility and the strange instinct to reach the clouds.

She immediately opened her eyes and pulled up her head; the last time, those clouds had put her in the hospital.

"You can't! I'm really going crazy!"

#

That evening Martina got back to the square. Her friends waiting for her, ran to meet her.

They wanted to know how it happened; each gave his opinion, and everybody were agreed to call it a strange paranoia that can sometimes happen. As demonstration, each person told of similar.

Martina listened to the stories, looking to herself as a plausible cause to the problem.

Daniel, however, was worried, and did not try to hide it: she was silent and paid attention to the friends' stories but was unconvinced.

The celebrations for her return had a normal ending next to the church, the group locked in a circle passing a big joint made by the most expert. Martina jumped her turn; she did not feel ready yet to resume; more important was to feel the presence of friends. After the days in hospital and those to follow, she felt weak, and not only physically. It was nice to be back together at home, in the main square, with houses around the church, the people on the bus—even their looks of contempt were reassuring.

Martina drew a long breath, she felt better.

Some pigeon was shuttling from the statue in the fountain to the roof of the church and down to the cobblestones, looking for something to eat, than resumed flight. The bird were chasing each other, sometimes pushing to be first to eat, sometimes challenging each other in strange attitudes.

A pigeon more strong than the others lorded his strength, running fast from the church to the fountain and scaring any other bird in his path.

Another smaller pigeon seemed indifferent to the bullying; he was quiet, looking in the folds of the pavement without notice the threatening rival. When the bully was near, it dropped a peck on the smaller bird's neck.

"Haii!" Martina screamed, touching her neck with her hand. The boys stopped their conversations to look at her. "That wretch of a pigeon thinks can rule over all! See how he attacked that other!"

The boys spied the center of the square. Somebody stood up to see better—they could not understand what had happened.

Martina searched through all the birds for the poor attacked pigeon; he had run away. She searched from the fountain to the floor, to the roof.

"Where is he? He will hurt the poor little pigeon!"

She continued her frenetic search, and her friends were watching her, worried—someone stood up, going away shaking his head. Martina, without noticing them, kept trying. She finally found him huddled in a corner near the church door, looking around, terrorized.

"He gave him a peck," she said, turning to Daniel, now

the only interlocutor. "There's been bad, poor pigeon! He can't even think of revenge; he does not feel strong enough—look!"

Daniel, stunned, looked at her.

"What's the matter with you, Martina—are you okay?"

She looked from the pigeon up at him. The question had come like a flash of clear sky in the middle of a huge storm, or as a black cloud in the middle of a deep blue sky. It made its space into Martina's head, slowly dodging other thoughts one by one, until it became the most important.

The girl became silent, meeting Daniel's worried face; she had been taken away unconsciously again.

"Do you see? I'm going crazy; I also speak with the pigeons now. What's happening to me?" She lowered her head.

"What's happening to me?"

#

In the following days Martina had other crises, one of which, more than the others, brought her back to the hospital again. And this second time brought the same rites of distrust and disbelief from the doctors.

Daniel took her to the hospital; they did not listen to his explanations. As a witness, he was not considered very reliable.

Another time mom and sergeant Panebianco came to visit her. Again they sat beside the bed in disbelief to see her, just a few days later, still in the same condition.

Martina could not understand; there must was a way to oppose this mind's tendency to run away. Maybe she should kept her mind busy in something: a hobby, a job, or something else. Maybe it was already time to leave the square and begin to become a serious person.

When she was left the hospital, the problem did not degreased. Sometimes she seemed to be successfully resisting and then took a little confidence, but her imagination was to punish her when she took a little courage.

Her illness was different from all the others. Not caught in weakness or moments of discomfort, it came in quiet moments, ready to punish at the first hint of optimism.

Martina no longer tried to conceal her problem as she did at the beginning. Everyone knew, and most of them avoided her for fear of being somehow involved.

Only Daniel, undaunted, continued to be near her. Once he said if was possible would gladly take upon himself a bit of her pain.

Someone suggested decisive action against it. She had to face the illness head on, meet it firmly. As someone who had nearly drowned, she must immediately run to jump into the sea to conquer her fear—so she would have to put herself again in the same night conditions at the park.

At first she drove out the thought of such a terrible event, but then, after having tried everything, she was convinced that she had no alternative. How could she continue to live in that way, to defend her sanity? She had become too weak; in a short time, she would collapse. They would find a split between body and mind, with Martina completely crazy.

She had no intention of ending up in that way—it was much better to rick attempting a cure. If she lost, her death would erase any agony.

CHAPTER SEVEN

The morning was already advanced; the sun was carrying its light through the window illuminating the fun patterns on the walls around her bed. She was woken up by a knock at the door. Ginetta was entering into the room, carrying the breakfast tray. The heat rose with sinuous clouds of steam over her head that soon dissipated.

She came forward slowly, checking her balance. At last she leaned over the bed. They were both silent, looking each other in the eyes. Ginetta twitched, and the smile faded immediately. Something had happened to the girl, she realized from Martina's terrified gaze.

She lowered her head.

"Why so fast? They just needed to run this way?"

Martina did not know what to say; tears in her eyes, her gaze instinctively fled the room's drawings, their merriment didn't belong.

"I don't know! I have such a mess, my life is so terrible, full of pain, and then the strange disease. I don't know how far has this brought me!"

"Strange disease?" asked Ginetta. "What strange disease are you talking about?"

Martina hastened to tell the square story. The woman listened, alternating facial expressions. More than heartbroken, she seemed surprised. She did not seem to understand Martina's pain and the devastation caused by her strange disease.

Meanwhile, the sun coming through the window was exploring most of the room. It had been from the head of the bed to the back wall, and from the high corner it was coming down against the wall.

Ginetta hesitated, uncertain about how to express herself. She seemed to struggle to refrain from speaking freely. Several times she had been about to start, but always bowed her head, as if giving up.

At last she decided. "No, I was not ready for that! I could not expect such a reaction. But how is this possible? A disease!" She got out of bed, turning her gaze from the opposite side; her hands, rising and falling quickly beat against her legs and made noise.

"Do you think this would be a disease? But then, how can you think that? A disease, then this! A disease!"

Ginetta seemed angry, went to the window, and leaned on the windowsill looking out. Silence fell again, indistinguishable to Martina. She didn't know what she was thinking and what she was answering.

Surely Ginetta had not understood Martina's suffering. What could she know of the long pain's months? She, so quiet up here on the mountains—what could she understand about the hard life out there, between so many people, in a city full of sadness, fear, and absurd thoughts?

What could she know about so terrible a loneliness, when no one can understand your problems?

Ginetta turned quickly, looking at her sternly. "Do you really think I don't know sadness, pain or nightmares? You are telling me about loneliness, but have you ever experienced the true loneliness? A solitude as long as eternity? You wait for somebody still thinking about you, for at least, in the background of their thoughts, a small memory of you be still survives. Cure this slim hope how you can cure a flower hanging from the ledge against the winter onslaught: throw it out of your mind, with the certainty that it no longer stands a chance!

"Now think about this waiting. Imagine it as the only reason for your life, and tell me if you really think I do not know loneliness?"

From talking so animatedly from the window, Ginetta had slowly approached Martina until she was in front of her.

Martina's mouth hung open in amazement. Ginetta had answered to her silent thought, not a question.

"How did you answer to my unspoken question?" she said, smiling surprise.

"About loneliness?" asked Ginetta, whispering. She had realized her error.

"Yes, I did no question about it; I was just thinking."

The woman was silent.

"You read my mind—it's so or, you just guessed?"

Ginetta seemed troubled and remained silent, but the absence of her denial placed Martina in a difficult situation. From the first moment, she had imagined Ginetta knew a lot about her situation; she had done everything possible to get the information out of Ginetta. In the mornings, coming in with a tray, it seemed Ginetta had understood everything.

Every relationship with Ginetta was destined to change if her mind was an open book.

The woman had always seemed to understand her doubts; she would raise her head and smile, a strange smile, which became even more strange when Martina found it inside her thoughts. There Ginetta's smile was an immediate and understandable as the image that in the mind produces a scent, like distant memories when they become so close that it seems they happened just the day before.

"I can hear you," said Martina.

Ginetta smiled. "So do you think this is a disease?"

Martina was confused and uncertain; it was hard not to believe Ginetta when the woman was, so close to her own thoughts.

"I really wanted it to be different and quietly stay here. Instead, you immediately took the road to the city. I would had taken you by the hand, made you understand how much the imagination can free your state of mind, and what thought can do if properly guided. Thought can get where you want. To heaven, if you want, or in a darker misery, if you think there might be and you are afraid—terrible nightmares in a living hell.

"The imagination is a tool—a great and powerful tool to use, just like a musical instrument, that can lead to a better tune or to a grating shiver. There, you have found yourself, and with this revelation comes a weapon powerful enough to bring your own destruction. How many people crashed from an interpretation error... I'd follow you to teach you how to use thought, so you would understand."

She heaved a long sigh, looked the girl in the eyes, and shook her head slowly.

"Now you feel ill with a disease difficult to treat, and you're right! That virus is inside you, ready to hit you every time your thought will try to get rid of it. Like a river breaking its banks when creating a new direction for the current, every drop of water seems to have an instinct to follow the open gate, there is no way to stop its descent.

"Inside you the levees broke; you will come to discover the mood of unimaginable terror. No need to hide—try not to think about them, they'll press you closely. They will always be next to you in life and in death."

Martina shuddered at such a definition of her illness; even death would not make her free.

"Oh yeah; the terror does not end when the body is no

longer able to contain life. The terror will continue to haunt you until you fight it again, and defeat it. There is no agreement possible, it lives and multiplies itself in uncertainty and bargaining...

"Wherever you go, if you want to live in peace, you need to go down again in that park, and face your fear and your defeat."

Martina was terrified at the thought of going back there; it would cause terrible nightmares. She began to sweat. Ginetta resumed the soft tones; her face was sad and melancholy.

"This is not what I had imagined for you. It was enough that to have only a little help and a bit of peace. You would have been able to understand how important the imagination inside your thoughts is. You would have learned to use it, just as a musical instrument can be used to bring out the best melody. So we could play together again as it once was!"

The word *play* made Martina smile; it seemed strange and out of place.

Ginetta smiled back.

"...Children's play is like a poem; as the most beautiful song ever written, like love feel when it moves. Children's play is pure imagination, emanating, without limitation. Their game led, without any effort, to overcome all the body and time barriers. The child has no uncertainty, no defenses to be raised, and knows no fears if someone else don't point them out. Instead, time and needs destroy the imagination.

"Have you never seen kids playing—their eyes, their face when they release their imaginations? Whatever they imagine becomes real. Then a stick can be a sword or, as in fairy tales, a pumpkin can become a coach.

"Tell me, Martina," she asked in a low voice, "what are your dreams? What could be now the most wonderful feeling in you? What could make you happy now?"

Martina was not ready for such a question. What could

be a happier dream than to be away from time, beyond needs? She searched for something more but kept finding situations too close to those constraints—intense feelings, but still too close to needs.

"I knew it, you can't find an answer!" Said Ginetta. "You've forgotten true joy. You were so busy defending your little state of mind from all fears that you become a slave. You can't remember what is and what was once a real joy for you. How I would have loved to try again, together, as when you were teaching joy to me."

Martina, incredulous, smiled. "When was it ever?" Ginetta smiled.

"It was a long time ago... or maybe just yesterday..."

#

She was still wondering what could give rise to the most wonderful feeling not related to time and needs, when thoughts from Ginetta prevailed in her head, so intense as to fully occupy her understanding. This time, Martina did not oppose; she squinted to better see the pictures.

Ginetta was sitting on the bed next to the girl, talking with in silence: the unspoken thoughts seemed a whisper. "It can happen, but it happened a long time ago in a small country town not far from a city. Small houses, almost united, keep each other company; there was a four-way crossing that ended in many white gravel walks into the country. Willow trees, in the evening when the sun goes down, seem to speak with the inhabitants of the ditches. Close to the village run two railroad's tracks, preserved by weeds and brambles."

Martina occasionally opened her eyes and looked at the woman; she did not understand what a strange kind of story they were telling themselves; to Martina it seemed one of those stories to tell children to make them sleep. The images in her head came clear and seemed to live among the few houses in the surrounding countryside, near the railway. Even Martina, when a child, had the railroad not far from her home.

"White clouds colored and filled the sky. From the mountains a bigger cloud, towering, brightly colored, seemed to be supported with an eye toward the plains to control other, smaller clouds, like a good mother. Every time the sun passes over, the light made it glow with a thousand colors.

"A child stood leaning against a willow tree, waiting. He was just waiting for the right moment; soon he'd run through the fields, jumping ditches. Waiting for the whistle of the train, he'd run fast to see the trains down there, near the old crossing. He'd rely on the crossing bars."

Martina was confused by the images, the familiar sense they expressed. Nothing else seemed important at this moment. How far was her life there in the city, a nightmare, a sad fact that didn't belong to her anymore.

The story was filling her mind; she saw the country, the countryside, and the railway as if she had always lived there. She could feel the smell of green born from the earth and manure. The railway and the train whistle approaching.

"He was waiting for freight trains, those long, endless wagons processions, all the same. He would have counted every component of that row, the cars like so many people holding hands, their slow, rhythmic noise relaxing the procession like a September fog.

"Before the level crossing, the train would give a loud and tender whistling, as when at night it fills the loneliness and casts out fear. He would lean his head and hands on the level crossing bars, dreaming one day to go up onto the cars for a long and endless journey. Far, far away, following the slow flow and rhythm of the wheels over the tracks. He would dream of an old train compartment, a wooden polished seat, his hands and chin against the window to admire the scenery scrolling just like an old movie, the countryside, the hills and mountains. He would wait after the last gallery, until the blue of the sea filled the window, its foaming waves like a smile, the smile of the sea…"

"The locomotive is coming from a distance; it's a confused image on the horizon taking shape slowly in the dark contours to become well-defined then—"

Martina, without realizing it, was continuing the story. The words following her imagination. Her fantasy had come to life: the images were sharp, freshly emerged from her thoughts, docile and ready for any mutation.

Ginetta let the girl's thoughts flow.

"Yes, it's a beautiful sunny day, and the boy is now ready, with all fingers raised as an abacus, to count the wagons. He's afraid of being confused; what if he can't remember the numbers sequence? One day or another would come a convoy with at least one more car. Until now he had come to count only to fifty…

"A noise propagates in the air, before the whistle then, with a shudder, the roar announced in advance by a strong wind, as a storm beginning. The locomotive and the first car whizzes past, forcing him to turn his head away for a moment. One, two, three… six, seven…

His hands are open, and the fingers are closing at the same rhythm for each car. Ten… No more fingers are left open to count with; with his left foot, he makes a mark in the sand, and his fingers are straight up again."

Ginetta was silent; she looked at the girl and her smiling face. Martina also, leaned against the crossing bars and seemed to be counting the train cars.

"In the sand strips are now four and his fingers are all closed. Forty-eight, Forty-nine, Fifty. The train is finished, just a small car, smaller than any other, is attached to the last, like a child running to stay with her mother. A small appendage in trouble to keep up with all the others: Fifty-one!

"His arms are raised with joy. Fifty-one! Finally, fifty-one! He runs along the tracks to see the train leave and his little wagon. His hands shaking, he jump for joy and greets the train riding to another world, the other world awaited for long time…

"One day, I will go up on that train; I will go away far, far away!"

For a moment, in Martina's eyes was the image of the train moving away, with its swish and constant motion. She also wanted to be on that train, follow that rhythm, tune it to her mind. Slowly she would fall asleep next to the window and leave the landscape lights to run discreetly without disturbing the harmony of a warm sleep.

"The train has passed, nobody now is next to the level crossing, maybe tomorrow yet again…"

Martina opened her eyes, coming back in the room at the farm.

Ginetta watched her and dreamily smiled, her eyes twinkling. "For a moment you were just you, who I knew a long time ago!"

Even Martina smiled.

#

Down there in the city, Martina instead was always more frightened. Sergeant Panebianco convinced her to go to a doctor, one he knew, a psychologist who listened attentively to her problems.

He told her not to worry; these things happen to many people in different ways. It was the cumulative effect of all the smokes consumed in many years. The mind is affected. She could be saved just by changing her life, studying, and take care to keep the mind occupied. She would have to change friends and maybe find a guy with whom to think about the future. In the end, the nightmares would go away, vanished in the same way they had come.

Changing life and changing friends was not so difficult; she had already abandoned most of them, as she could no longer follow their lifestyle. She had become an unexpected girl, halfway between them and something impossible to define.

For some time, after her talks with the psychologist, her mind seemed back to normal. It did not seem so hard to restrain herself; she was able to avoid involving herself in certain situations. She began to go out at night; sometimes even her smile seemed sincere.

One evening in December, a few days before Christmas, the square was filled with pine trees. They were still bare of the lights that should be put on soon.

Martina was sitting, wrapped in a jacket and a scarf through which one could see only her eyes and nose.

Suddenly she felt a strange sensation in her body; perhaps the closeness of the festivities, the frenzied sense across the square, people, parcels, children like ping-pong balls bouncing around their mothers.

There was a sense of expectation in the air, that feeling she loved when as child. That sense came back with the memory of the Christmas Eve in the old house outside the city—the gifts waiting and all the poetry of the party; the father, mother, and all the relatives with different expressions.

She saw the same excitement in the children's eyes around the square and the joy of their mothers.

She felt a lump of envy and unhappiness in her throat, an envy and unhappiness feeling. When would never be able to get rid that weight? Would she wait like everyone else on Christmas with shopping trips, in the midst of the light, choosing small gifts for friends? Would she choose the funniest, already starting to laugh imagining the face of who would have received? And then the children, the music, the tinkling ornaments hanging on the tree.

Martina smiled sadly, eyelashes hidden a scarf. She had not realized it, but she had inadvertently given way to thoughts, and the imagination was driving her with nostalgia to that preferred party. She saw her childhood:

the preparations, the gifts waiting: seeing her mother's eyes became strangely cunning, and mother's constant questions about whether she was good or not this year.

Her mother laughed at her every 'yes,' at every confirmation that, despite its faults, this year the gifts would arrive.

Where did all this poetry go? Could she still be living a life without even a little poetry?

The tears flowed without her crying; she was as bare as the trees. Her bared soul, sad and empty, was unable to feel happy emotions, forced to amorphous stability so as not to meet the nightmares. At the first tear, she began to gasp for breath. Still she cried slowly, without despair, with sadness, as her whole life had been one continuous, slow tear.

Her life had been reduced to a kind of survival, the instinct to go ahead. Another hiccup stumbled on breath.

Her heart began to pound.

The square was filling up with people, but none of her friends where around. If only there was somebody beside her, she could talk of other questions and wouldn't have to chase the oddities in her head.

A black dog, old in his gait, slowly approached the pines, sniffing fairly calmly, and seemed to complain about his old age. The dog lay down next to the huge trees.

Somebody did not find the situation appropriate and chased him away. The dog sniffed Martina and lay down. For a moment, their eyes met.

"You and I are same—can't have a party!"

The old dog let out a large yawn and crouched down next to her. Together they stood looking at the square. She wanted to comfort him, talk to him, and tell him that the people were not all so cruel. But no one could console her of those thoughts that were shaking in her head; it was too late. Her mind was shaking; would never be able to stop it.

"I am lost; it's happening again!" She put her head in her hands, covering her eyes, she wanted to be at home, not here. That square was no longer her home. She tried to chase away all the sad impressions; but knew she had no chance.

A few minutes later, after an unequal fight, she fell, unconscious to the ground.

\#

Martina left the hospital only a week later, together with Daniel. This time her fainting in the square had made headlines, and also a small space on the city newspaper.

They walked slowly along the road back home. Martina was sadder than usual. "I feel missing strength. I have to do absolutely something to get out. I have to do it now; otherwise, never more. The will is fading. Soon I will be sure that this is my natural state; I will accept being crazy! I don't want that do happen! I thought a lot these days when I was in the hospital bed, and I decided! One of these days I'll do it again!"

"You'll what?" asked Daniel, worried. He walked beside her on the way home.

"One of these days I'll do it again. I will get somewhere; I'll smoke a joint, and I'll be waiting. If it's fate should I become crazy or die, I don't want go ahead this kind of agony. I can't live a life like this…"

She gave a long sigh; her gaze was turned toward the ground. "But if there is a chance, a way out, I want to try. If go wrong, at least I'll finish suffering. A life in this way does not make sense."

They walked slowly, Daniel shivering to hear her determination.

"You know, I've tried everything, I followed the advice of all. I waited to let time take away my paranoia; however, my mind is able to regenerate fears, and always brings me new ones. I tried, and I feel I have no alternative."

Daniel tried to dissuade her. He reminded her of the psychologist advise; sooner or later its crisis would be gone, and at last just it would be only a bad memory.

Martina looked at him with affection. "Please; if I wait again, I might make other decisions, much more drastic. At this point the idea of taking my own life is not as hard as it would be to continue. I want relief; this is my last chance!"

She flatly refused to be accompanied. The prospect of being rescued in the middle of a crisis; would invalidate her decision. She wanted to be alone, without any help, and with the real possibility of dying. Only in this way could she get out.

In the following months, she was twice close to doing it but lacked the courage. She always kept a piece of chosen smoke collected in a box above her bed. Occasionally, she looked at it, sooner or later would take it.

In June, after another crisis, she closed her eyes, took the piece of Hashish, put it in her pocket, and left the house by herself, heading toward the square.

#

She walked slowly up to the tree-lined square and stood around watching. Some of her friends were laughing in a circle.

She remembered her first time, and how it was hard to get close to them. How she had waited and suffered for such a decision! She had been sure she would not be accepted. Now was the farewell moment; whatever happened, it would not be the same again.

Taking a side street, she passed the square. The wind was blowing even when Martina turned on the right onto a narrow alley. It was known as a place where all the junkies wanted to shoot up. No one ventured down there; it was just the smell that emanated.

It was a very narrow road; no cars could pass; the sides were high walls, dark at the base and becoming shiny as they gradually rose up. At the top, the sun made its appearance. After a few steps down the alley, she turned left, went on for about thirty feet to come to another wall. At that point the smell was unbearable; it seemed the beginning of hell. On the ground there were syringes and pieces of rags soaked with blood.

Martina avoided a strong impulse to leave; if not now, would never have the courage.

She pulled out a cigarette from the pocket, broke it in half, threw away most of the tobacco, put down a small amount in a little foil, took the piece of smock, and heated it with the a lighter flame. When everything was hot, she mixed it with tobacco, which she poured into a tobacco paper that she rolled up and licked the edge, where there was the glue. The result was a small, white cone.

Martina took the lighter, hesitated for a moment, put the joint in her mouth, lit it, and took a long drag.

The smoke and its flavor travelled down into her lungs; she had to suppress the urge to vomit. She inhaled deeply a second and a third time.

The joint was half gone, the red embers had taken the place of the tobacco paper.

Martina took two more long drags. At the end, she threw the butt on the ground and snuffed it with her shoe.

"It's done!"

She walked near the wall, leaning back, and slowly descended to sit on the step of a walled-up door a long time ago.

Her mind was still clear, far from the first effect, that calm euphoria forgotten. She felt only fear, which would soon come to a crisis as the first bolt of a big storm.

She felt something in her stomach, a whirlpool twisting and slowly turning. It was the first symptom. The reeling increased to occupy most of her stomach. She could see just by closing her eyes: the image was dark gray, like jelly, in an edible form. Starting from the center, a spiral widened, losing itself against the walls of the stomach. When she approached the walls, a pulse rose to the brain.

The first pulse reached the brain, then a second and a

third. The reel increased intensity and speed and the pulses became more frequent.

Suddenly the whole mass broke, going in a single movement to her head. The explosion made her head move as after a slap. Only a few seconds followed by another pulse more powerful than the first. Martina followed them one by one, her heart pounding.

"No! No!"

Along with the arrival of pain, her mind began to go away; it seemed to her the size of the alley had deformed. It seemed an endless corridor, a huge highway of bloody syringes, rags thrown on the ground, and unbearable smells. The houses' walls had become huge enclosures from which she could not escape. Behind her, the way by which she had arrived no longer existed; in its place was a huge crevasse.

This new dimension seemed to make her sway as if her head was under blows. There was no chance to ask for help; she was too weak to make any decision.

She closed her eyes clutched her head with her hands, than squeezed until it hurt. Her stomach hurt; she wanted to throw up but could not.

The houses' walls were bent; the tops of the roofs came down to touch her head. The sparrows, jumping from rooftop to rooftop, seemed hawks ready to pounce on her.

Martina, clutching her head, hugged herself so hard that she began to prevail over the pain.

Hugged, hugged…

\#

The clouds broke their story, leaving Martina distraught and surrounded by uncertainty. No other cloud told of her life in the square.

She peered around the prairie; and frantically analyzed the clouds.

There was nothing else left of her life. The memories

were interrupted at that point, like a book in the middle of the narrative, or a movie when its film breaks and events remain suspended in the middle.

Martina panicked. "Then I'm dead!" She looked around scared.

#

This time it was Martina who woke up Ginetta at dawn.

Together they went up slowly up the hill, through the woods, making their way through the animals heedless of their presence. They walked silently round the hills full of soft grass and sat down under the tree.

"You come to the end of your trip!" Ginetta said, smiling. "I have so much hoped to have you here for a while, but the events have been hammering away in a hurry; now you're going away!"

"Then I'm not dead?" asked Martina, Ginetta shook her head, smiling. "No, you're not dead!"

"If I'm not dead, where do I go?"

To this question Ginetta did not answer; instead, she lowered her gaze. Martina immediately realized her destiny.

"I have to go back there—yes?"

Ginetta nodded.

"You can't mean that! Do you really mean I have to come back another time, there in the alley?"

Ginetta nodded again. "You did not ever go away from that alley! You were always there; you're even there now!" Ginetta looked up staring at the clouds. She didn't have the courage to face Martina. Where would she would find the strength to come out unhurt from a test so devastating? Martina was so weak and helpless, like a leaf, long battered by a storm, swinging on the branch, clinging to life only with its last hold.

The girl's fate was being decided without any remedy. Ginetta had to let her go without other possibilities. "You have to go now; your time is over—you will soon find that you are no longer here and maybe there never have been..."

Martina apprehensively listened.

"You will not be able to slow the momentum; it will be like a strange wind will pull you away. The memory of me and this place suddenly will be full of doubt and uncertainty, like a blur, a dream soon to be forgotten."

Ginetta lowered the head again. "You've been too little here with me; we could have dreamed, as then—so much fun. Instead..."

The clouds streamed across the sky, slowly pushed by the wind. The sun was hidden behind them, just to reappear soon after, as if it were playing hide-and-seek.

Martina looked at the clouds; she felt Ginetta speaking slowly, but the woman's words began to lose their meaning.

Martina was taken away by the dynamism of their flow. She seemed to be one of them.

Then she could not even hear Ginetta's words; it seemed a strange wind had stolen the noise and carried it far, far away.

Now before her eyes was a huge blue sky and a continuous noise, dense and attractive. She smiled, drifting.

Everything seemed to be finished.

CHAPTER EIGHT

Feeling she was back in the alley, in the middle of the smell and in the midst of the crisis, was a terrible feeling. Martina panicked. It had seemed to be somewhere else. Instead...

She was sitting on the steps; her fingers still smelled of the flavor of the joint. Even a few seconds seemed to be spent in an indefinable duration of a dream.

She felt her head and whole body immersed in terrible pangs. She still was looking at the blue sky, clouds flowing, with the words of Ginetta wandering in her head in a one long and incomprehensible sound—a strange and unattainable dream, strongly opposed to its current state.

Such thoughts would have her wake up in her bed, sitting with her eyes closed in a little daydreaming. She relived every moment, closed her eyes, and pretended that she was not back yet. She kept that daydream bound tightly to her throughout the day a situation that gave her serenity.

Instead there was the alley, the smell and the feeling of being in the antechamber of hell. It had been only a dream, the effect of deviance, a strange imaginative twist. The mind, for protection, had gone to take refuge far away, in search of some relief.

Her slip back here to the alley, however, had a devastating effect, as a disease that manifests more powerful after its relapse. For a few seconds, she had been immersed in a strange calm, a feeling of well-being that bordered oblivion. She had imagined a different world, a place where she can be in peace, away from all the problems, in perfect harmony! But fate was to be just that, if, in the midst of the most fantastic dream, she had ended up returning here.

#

Slowly she began to cry, a crying without consolation— a slow way down in hopeless tears, sad, without a way out.

Away, out of the alley, bouncing off the walls in strange echoes came the muffled sounds of traffic. She felt it was a different world—a sort of intermediate situation, so far from her life.

She restrained the urge to escape and return to normal life, even though the pain was unbearable. She was going to get to the bottom. She did not want to go back to the hospital and resume everyday life alternating nightmares with the expectation of other nightmares.

The blasts in her head were terrible; she felt struck by a strange and powerful force. She held her head and pressed hard, so the physical pain would be more bearable, replace the thoughts.

"What the hell's wrong with you?"

She whirled; a few steps ahead, a guy was watching her. Martina dropped her hands from her head, looked up, grinned, then again squeezed her head with her hands. The boy pressed again.

"Hey, I'm talking to you! What's going on?"

Martina shook her head; perhaps this strange boy was

part of a nightmare.

"These are not things that concern you; go away! Can't I be alone even in the most disgusting place in the city? Must there always be somebody asking questions?"

The boy seemed unimpressed by Martina's grumpy ways and continued to observe with curiosity.

"You're not fine at all!"

"Oh really?" thought Martina sarcastically. For a moment, just for a moment, she was able to smile.

"If you want to help somebody, it is better go somewhere else; I do not want your help. I just want to be left alone!"

There was a long silence. The boy kept at a little distance, without going away. His gaze seemed surprised, and not at all worried about a sad and painful situation. He was still motionless in front of her; he thinks he wanted to understand the situation.

"But really, how do I tell you to go away?"

She rose unsteadily, clutching the wall, her head swaying like a drunk.

"I want to be left alone! Do you understand?"

"Yes, sure, yes, I understand, I'm not stupid! I understand, you want to be left alone."

The boy smiled, looking carefully at the girl, and discerning her attitudes.

"So?" Martina asked again.

"So what?" said the boy.

She spread her arms and turned away, discouraged.

"You can't. I took all of a lifetime to be brave to come here, the farthest and most disgusting place in the world, sure that no one will ever find me. But no! Here too, there is someone!" She cursed, gesturing. "I don't want a hand from anyone; I want to be left alone! Do you understand or not?"

The boy waited for a moment and seemed to consider with a long internal argument, the girl's question, before giving the answer.

"No!"

"No what?" Martina asked incredulously.

"No, I do not want to leave! I want to stay here!"

"This is just stupid!" Martina whispered, stretching out her arms, leaning against the wall, letting go as if to fall until she found herself sitting on the steps again with her hands clutching her head. Tried to chase the idea of someone standing near.

The flashes in her head continued undeterred.

Silence back to the alley. Martina was sitting, and the boy was still in same place, closely watching without interfering. His face changed expression, as he evaluated the girl's attitude, following every movement of her head. He stretched out his neck, trying to find a gap in her hands to see her face.

Martina felt his presence as a rock, as if thousands of people were looking at her, judging her actions. She expected at any moment to be seized and forcibly carried away. She would cry, writhing, would reach more people and an ambulance, and then away again to the hospital for another of her steps in grief.

Each time it happened, nothing had changed. She would be reestablished for a few days, maybe a few weeks, until the next crisis.

But there passing minutes, the wait was more strange and tense; she could not understand what was going on and what were the intentions of the strange boy.

She freed her head from her hands. Nobody was standing in front of her; she turned her head one way then the other.

She winced when saw the boy's head a few inches from her. He sat down beside her. His gaze was so close to getting inside her head. She jumped up, moving to the side, and looked at him with terror. "Can I know what you want?"

"I... nothing, I want nothing! What about you?"

Martina was visibly upset. "What I want should not be

of interest to you. Who are you? What are you doing here? Why don't you go somewhere else? Do you want money for hole?"

She checked into her pockets for some money, but nothing came out except a handkerchief. The boy instead quiet smiled, without moving an inch from her side.

"I don't have money, even other stuff. I had only a joint but I'm sorry, I've already smoked; I have nothing interesting for you, so go away!"

The boy was oblivious to the wrath of Martina. His face was not even trying to hide the pleasure of being there.

Martina bent her head again, trying to forget the uncomfortable companion by her side. The boy was always beside her, following every twitch of pain.

"I know your name," he said suddenly, turning for a moment to look elsewhere.

Martina heard those words as though they were coming from another world.

"Your name is Lilla!"

That name sounded strange. He had certainly mistaken her for another, so perhaps this was the reason he had not yet gone away. If she had not been in so difficult a condition, the situation would be very funny.

"Lilla" she thought... What a strange name! She didn't know anybody with that name. But it was not entirely unknown; she probably had already heard that name. Indeed, she was sure, but she couldn't remember where she'd heard.

The pain and the nightmares kept possession of her mind, and that strange name would not go away, remaining stuck in a corner of her mind and waiting, as an unexpected guest sits in the corner at a party waiting for the right moment to approach.

It was not just a curiosity; there was also a strange feeling bound to that name.

"Lilla," she whispered slowly, so that the sound of the

word would help her remember when and where she had heard it before. But the result of the research was only a vague feeling of well-being, nothing else.

She spoke again that name and stood waiting.

That name contrasted with flashes in her head and continued undeterred despite their rhythm destruction, but their vehemence seemed to decrease. A small part of her mind was busy trying that name.

"Martina! Martina is my name, not Lilla!" She said, showing for the first time a faint smile. She had been peeping through her hands.

She had better watch the boy although a bit scruffy, he did not look like a junkie. Who knows what was he doing in the alley dedicated to them.

He remained silent, with no strange moves. Usually everyone in such a situation, if they didn't find the courage to personally help a person in need, quickly came to call someone else.

It was really strange attitude, a kind of game. The pain was like a fiction that he refused to believe, or like many imaginary diseases that vanish when someone finds reason to laugh about them.

"No, your name is Lilla! To me you always been... Lilla." "Lilla's weeping willow!"

Martina winced at the image of the willow.

"Sorry, did you say—?"

"You are Lilla! Lilla's weeping willow!"

The girl was confused; she could not make sense of this new idea; even the lightning stood aside to make space for this new and strange situation.

"So who are you?" She asked nervously.

"I am Edi!"

Martina stood for a moment, looking at him with her mouth wide open. Edi instead smiled happy.

"You're—Edi?"

The boy nodded, spreading his arms.

"Here I am!"

"But you can't! You can't be here! You are part of—"
The phrase jammed; she could not define which part he
was a part of. "You don't really exist, just do part of my
imagination! I'm still dreaming, or maybe I've already gone
mad!"

Edi smiled. He looked at Martina, not caring of her
words; rather it was her eyes, the way she moved, rather
than the words she has saying that was attracting his
attention.

Martina didn't added more. How could speak with a
piece of dream—with somebody who should not have
been there? She walked slowly to see if was just a picture,
one of many hallucinations. Her index finger was stretched
out with the intention of touching his shoulder. She
touched it as if with the fear of electric shock.

Both smiled, and Edi said, "I've been down here
waiting for you all this time; I was afraid of not being able
to get hold of you. I was afraid to leave you alone in your
greatest time of need. I knew it: you should've come here
to finish your trip!"

"My trip?"

#

She could not utter more except than truncated
sentence.

She was confused; everything was happening so fast—
as if by magic, the thoughts in her head had turned docile.
The blasts suddenly stopped, and her stomach had
stopped pushing to come out.

As in an early and sudden spring after a long winter,
Martina seemed to wake up from a nightmare. She
touched her head and didn't feel even the thick needles
stuck inside. Everything was gone; in their place was Edi
and his smile, that strange expression that filled her head
and drove her thoughts.

There was also the strange name: Lilla's weeping

willow, that evoke something, even if she did not remember ever having had heard the name before, not even as a joke when she was a child.

Edi watched her carefully; Martina felt his eyes penetrate her mind, slowly, without anxiety, like Ginetta's had. Still, she could not believe the nightmares' disappearance, suddenly and without a trace. In their place had entered Edi's mind, which had brought tranquility, and tamed the nightmares as the sudden arrival of the owner quiets guard dog.

"What has happened to you, Lilla? How did you reduce you so?"

Martina was uncertain; maybe it was not for him to judge her last years in the square.

"I'm not talking about the lifestyle that you have chosen," said Edi, anticipating the girl. " I'm talking about your head. How did you become so complicated? Didn't you see are drowning in a glass of water? It's Just you, that the seas parted to let you pass. How did it happen that your imagination has turned against you?"

Martina shook her head. "I was so bad!"

"I see it! I never thought one day to slow down your thoughts and put myself in your head so they don't hurt you! How strange, having to avoid your thoughts, ask them to step aside. Like asking a river in the desert to go somewhere else and let the green banks become dry!"

Martina would have left willingly so much initiative to exit healed from the alley and go home. Forget all the suffering caused by thoughts.

Instead, she imagined that soon, when Edi had gone away, everything would be back as before. The pain would have reduced her again so badly as to have to go into hiding.

Edi followed her thoughts.

"Like cats or dogs when they suffer, is not it, Lilla? When they feel the end, they go into hiding. Don't you remember the dogs, Lilla?"

"What have the dogs," Martina thought, "got to do with the nightmares?"

"You said you were like dogs and cats, which when terrified by danger, go into hiding. You said, that they keep their soul close because it won't not flee. In those moments, life is tied to a thin wire and can abandon them. You were holding your head, as if it might flee when you were afraid."

Martina followed Edi's words, unable to understand. "That afternoon, behind the gate near your home, Lillo was not there waiting for you. How many times have you rang the bell for him? You went around the country rummaging in every hole, calling with a loud voice, praying, crying to see him…"

Hearing Edi's words inside her, she suddenly remembered that dog. She had gone to greet every morning and in the afternoon often took him for a walk. It was the dog of the courtyard in a house not far from her house.

"Lillo was one of your favorite dogs; you never failed to greet him in the morning when you left the house to go to school.

"That morning, you found the empty courtyard; something must have happened to him. You went determined to the field behind your small town. His owners had not believed you when they reluctantly followed you looking into ditches in the countryside.

"Lillo was lying in pain that car had invested. You had heard… You were able to hear her moan."

Martina listened with wide eyes. It was her childhood he was talking about.

How the poor dog had suffered and all day she had watched beside the doghouse.

"He died in your hands, just when it seemed he could recover." His smile became compassionate. "Do you remember what you said the next day? When asked how did you know where Lillo was?…

Martina did not remember.

"He had told you, you said. He told you to run, because he felt pain."

In her mind, coming back, was Lillo's image: his large ears, hind legs a bit crooked, tongue always leaning forward, and eyes dark and deep.

"Now you get scared when thoughts create the imagination. That imagination that made you able to communicate with any living being."

Martina could not speak.

"Don't you remember his look? Don't you remember his eyes, Lilla? Throughout the day, you were there to caress his breath and count his heartbeats. His eyes seemed to be linked to your by an invisible thread. All day long he continued to look at you.

"Don't you remember how your favorite dog died, as the pain disappeared after his last breath? As you smiled and looked around, your favorite dog was no longer in his destroyed body, but had not even gone. He was still there next to you.

"How long have kept him with you, before letting him go? When he left, did you keep close at least the name, a symbol to remember? From that moment, to me you were always Lilla—Lilla's weeping willow!"

Silence fell in the alley; Edi watched Martina as she was immersed in memories. The emotion at remembering her favorite dog. She seemed to still see him at the gate, arriving on time every morning as she passed. His wagging tail, ears raised, and tip of his tongue outstretched to meet her nose.

Edi stared at her, when wanted to say something important, his eyes looked sad: even expressed a smile.

"Two are the lives, one living, one to be invented. The first one is often forced to live it as it comes. Sometimes you can change it, and then it seems everything works fine, but sometimes it does not work at all.

"But there is another life; it can lead you where anxiety doesn't exist, away from the nightmares. This life is not born when the body is born and does not end when you have to leave it. It is always there waiting for you.

"Death is a dam that stands along the river flowing. When you get close, everything seems to be finished; a huge obstacle with the power to stop the river. But then resumed, a little further downstream, the river again, with new sources, flows to meet its destiny.

"The imagination is able to raise the mind, above the usual optics. It leads up in the top of the highest mountain to discover the entire existence, without limitations—over the dam, over any barrier—the entire existence."

#

The two boys were sitting on the steps, side by side. Edi still held in check the thoughts in the mind of Martina. Her thoughts were restless, like wild horses waiting to spring forward together.

Martina was able to understand the importance of imagination and how much had been dominant during her childhood. But now she was no longer a child, and would not be back to childhood. She did not need that strength; it just complicated her life. What she needed now was quiet, like any other person being able to walk along the city streets without the fear of strange and enterprising thoughts suddenly taken away.

Could she sit in the square and watch the moon without danger? Wake up in the morning with the desire to get up and not with regret at being alive?

Edi comprised, as Martina had changed, that he could not blame her: he had not considered to be in front of a woman in crisis. He had to be strong enough to help her, not to return to the shelter, but to continue on her way.

"Don't worry; I will not push you to do things you're afraid of. It is my fault; I wish so much, my Lilla to forget you are no longer the same. After so many years, things have changed, and I have to know it. Up there at the shelter, time instead seems to never run, and probably us also with it. I had the presumption of wanting to join hands and bring you there, close to the willow."

Martina was lost; she felt Edi's sadness but could not do anything about it.

"You can go home without worrying about your illness, no longer hide, and look to the future without uncertainty. I'll go back up there taking away what's left of my Lilla. Me and Ginetta, we'll pretend you are still with us as it was then!"

Martina welcomed with happiness the news: the end of her nightmares! But she could not chase away a bit of sadness. She had to say good-bye to childhood imagination, to shelter, to the clouds. It was the price to pay to live on.

"Now I know; never return to us! I'm hurting, and there is nothing worse… Hurt to the people you care about."

His eyes were wet with tears.

"I know, it is to let you continue to live. But it is not simple: How to take away the wings to a bird, even if it is necessary to him to continue to live?"

Edi stood by the stone steps, sadly watching Martina.

"What will happen when a dam again shall stand before you, and you will have to deal with your real life? What will happen if the memory of the most beautiful Lilla goes away? I can't imagine that you can live again without the memory of what you were!"

His face became thoughtful, in front of a big question.

"I make you remember and understand what you've lost, so it remains vivid in your memory." He took her hand, squeezing it tightly in his. "This is my last gift in exchange for all yours!"

Edi held tight her hands and stared into Martina's eyes, because she agreed to another trip.

The girl looked at him with terror; he could not ask her so much. She tried to free her hands, but the force could also change her intentions. She restrained the impulse to withdraw, nodded with a smile, and relaxed her muscles.

Her head was filled with emotions, like the first time when found herself beside the willow.

Edi took away Martina to her childhood in order to remain attached in her memory. They went away together, leaving another Martina sitting on the steps, completely absent.

PART THREE

...the childhood

CHAPTER NINE

It was late in the afternoon; Martina was sitting outside the door of an old country house.

A farmer was coming out of a stable with a pitchfork resting on his shoulders, and she heard the cows' calls. He walked slowly, balancing the weight, some manure dropping from the end of the pitchfork. After a few steps, he stopped throwing everything into a pit already swollen with manure.

Martina, sitting on an old wooden chair, was watching the farmer's movements. The air was overfull with that pungency; the warm wind in the afternoon drove it to her with the cries of the hungry cows.

It was one of those summer afternoons when Martina spent a walk in the small town or on long walks in the countryside. But today was a sad day; she had no desire to go around. She was curled up in a chair by the door of the house.

Sometimes she could relax and her gaze, running along the courtyard, could give a reason to smile. Then, when she realized the reason for waiting, her face turned dark again, and she bent her head sadly.

Except for the farmer, no one could cross the yard; the sun seemed a sentry with a flaming sword in his hand, ready to strike anyone who ventured.

Three women on the opposite side of the porch were sitting facing each other, talking wildly, sometimes laughing. Their laughter seemed to dissolve in the heat of the afternoon. A little girl, out of a room after dodging the towel hanging on the door frame, offered a bit of water from a kettle. The three women smiled, took the ladle and drank in turn.

Martina kept looking around, but stayed seated, as if she were tied to the chair by an invisible thread. Her attention was soon stolen, by a hollow sound, startling her; she recognized the sound of an engine coming from outside the yard. She narrowed her eyes.

A red tractor, half rusty, was taken into the courtyard. The three women stopped talking, and each gave a nod. The farmer walked slowly across the yard and stood on the porch, next to the stables.

A man got out of the tractor, checked the engine, shook his head, then took off his hat and wiped his forehead. "I feel that soon it will forsake me," he said slowly, turning to the farmer, who was depositing more manure in the pit.

Martina watched with apprehension as her father coming forward after following behind the tractor. She bowed her head when he was near.

"We need to talk!"

Martina did not say a word. She looked down as if to avoid the impulse of the words.

"Wait here; now I'm coming!"

He entered the house without another word.

Martina put back her head back in her hands; her face had become dark again. She knew what to expect; she disobeyed again nonetheless. She didn't realize exactly how it had happened; it was just stronger than her.

She raised her eyes again.

An old dog, into the courtyard, moved up the steps slowly, as if trying to avoid the sun's rays. It was an old dog with his tongue hanging out, heavy at least as the years he carried below. Martina was near; a few steps in front of him, in the middle of the courtyard, under the sun, the dog sat as if waiting for an answer.

Martina looked around, worried, first to the colorful tent from which her father soon would come, then to the old dog, shaking her index finger at him. "I can't come with you today," whispered Martina, looking around. "I can't come anymore to play with you."

The dog let out a loud yawn, than lay on the ground with his nose in the middle of the front legs.

"Don't do that! You know, it's not my fault, I'll be pleased to come, but I can't. Soon will come Dad, and if he sees me here talking to you, it will be even worse. So go— come on, go away, please!"

The dog let out a snort, hesitated a moment, then stood up and walked over to the door. He turned back again, stopping and waiting.

Martina outstretched arm pointing to the door again. The dog turned onto the exit and walked away.

Martina put back her head in her hands. Soon would come her father.

#

"I'm sick of you! Tell me what to do to make you stop? I've tried everything. I tried hard for you to understand you don't do this!" The man was leaning against the door. He had a towel on his forehead, his short hair was pulled back, his eyes were fixed on her.

"You promised me, don't you remember? Just two days ago you promised me, and instead you did it again!"

"But, Dad," interjected Martina. "I didn't want to do this. I really didn't want to do—"

"Then why did you do it again?" he interrupted. "I stood at the window, and I saw you again talk to that damn dog. But how is this possible? I've never seen anyone daydreaming with a hairy face or"—the man, anguished waved his hands— "with any other living being on the earth. No child is lost as you get lost. You can't do like all your friends at school, playing with dolls or talking to each other. No you don't—you speak with the dogs! You go around the country to talk to the animals; what do people say? The others, when they meet me, smile and shake their heads. Have not you noticed? None of your friends are coming here to our home. Their parents don't allow them!"

"But Dad…" Martina, desperate, pleaded.

"You can't! It just had to happen to me: a child so strange! She wants to talk to the dogs!"

The man began to walk back and forth in a rage. He waved his hands as if to ward off a fate fallen apart.

"With the dogs! And with everything with which no living being would ever speak!"

He entered the house to come out soon after; in his hand he was still holding the towel, and he was still shaking his head. He spent a few seconds, which to Martina seemed like hours. She knew what would come immediately after his judgment against her.

Her suspicion was confirmed when her father began to speak:

"You know, now I have to punish you!"

Martina nodded, trying to show the most sad face to move him to compassion.

"I could beat you… forbid you to leave the house or keep studying for a whole month. But I'm sure it was not enough; you'd soon again disobey me!"

Her father's face had become very serious. Martina was worried about what punishment would be given to her.

"The punishment for you is much more terrible than you're thinking. You will remember for a long time! I will punish you in this way every time you disobey me! I'll find you in talking with the animals!"

He stopped for a moment before the verdict.

"You'll spend two hours every afternoon for a week locked in the broom closet! Even if you set out to cry and beg, I assure you, no one will open it up for you."

Martina feared that dark room without windows, only a little more than seven square feet. She had always avoided opening the door of that room, imagining terrible monsters inside. She would be afraid even when she saw the dark inside while mom had placed the brooms before closing the doors. She had imagined many times being inside, and each time she had chills.

Her father's judgment made her burst into tears.

"No, Dad... please... I promise, I will not anymore! But in the closet, no! I'm afraid... please, not in the closet!"

She took his hands, shaking. Her father had moved away, trying to keep his anger that was justifying that decision.

"No, this is the punishment that will be repeated each time, so you'll remember! I've decided!"

#

The first time he found his daughter in such an attitude he was not very worried: talking to a doll or to an animal in the street, there was not much difference. Her father and mother had smiled at Martina's imagination.

But then she began to be late for school and come home late, because she had stopped in the street for every animals. Often she came home with a dog or cat and began to cry every time to the poor animal was shown the exit.

Martina was always talking about her emotions; the delay to school was due because it was important to speak to all the animals she encountered. If she had left out someone, the next day he would put on a grudge because of jealousy. In the morning Martina started much earlier than other children, but she always arrived late to school.

Her father one day followed her secretly and saw her approaching the gate of a house while caressing a dog and talk to him closely.

"Hello Lillo! How are you today? Yes, I know, you're angry because I didn't take you on a walk yesterday, but it was Buio's turn; you had the day before—don't you remember?"

The dog wagged its tail; her father did not believe his ears when heard her daughter continue. "Are you sad today?"

She sat beside him and caressed the dog that answered her words by wagging his tail. She cuddled the furry snout, snapping a loud kiss near his big black nose.

He could not hear anything more; the voice of his daughter had become a whisper. She spoke as is to her best friend.

Her father had come home confused, undecided on what attitude to take. He did not want, with a punishment to create a problem. But after some time, Martina isolated herself from other children and constantly followed her strange predisposition.

She wandered around afternoons alone, accompanied by a dog, in the countryside. She sat with the dog on the edge of the ditches, and she was a long time splashing the water with a stick. Sometimes she would sit next to a tree and, completely thoughtful, watch the sky. She took the dead branches and built huts in which took refuge.

He watched the other children play together in the courtyard next to the house and looked with sadness at his daughter's situation. By now Martina was considered a problematic child, and no one wanted their children to play with her.

He was sure that Martina was special, but he preferred she be like the others, a normal child who enjoyed the quiet of her childhood and did not remain alone. Life, after childhood, already gives too much loneliness without looking for it at such a young age.

He was aware of his daughter's ability to communicate. When he was holding her hand going to town, it was as if Martina spoke; he felt her thoughts and mood without words.

Sometimes he observed that when she was asleep, it seemed she felt his presence. He wished to understand his daughter's thoughts, but he could not; it was too complicated.

He thought of Martina even when he was at work in the fields, comparing his childhood to that of his daughter. He too loved animals, but not like that.

There was a strange force stirring inside his daughter's head, stronger than her promises. They were sincere promises, but she could not keep them. After another promise, he had spied her walking down the street, looking forward with a firm resolve not to meet the eyes of the dogs behind the gates.

Sometimes she even put her hands, like blinders, on the sides of her face and walked briskly. But that lasted a short time; less than a quarter of a mile. Then she gradually slowed the pace till to stop, as if a dark force willed her to do so. She could not even get to the school, without stopping and talking with them and caressing their noses.

Another time he had followed his daughter after having threatened to not let her leave the house. She had traveled the road to the first intersection, stopped in the middle of the street, put her hands on hips, her face angry, and had shouted as if in front of an audience: "Stop it! I no longer have to keep calling. My father forbade me, and I can't be with you, you understand? Why do you still create me problems?"

The chickens and rabbits in the courtyards of all the area had a name, and she was despaired when she called them they ran away.

He chose that punishment as a last resort; certainly cruel, maybe it would leave an indelible mark on her life. Maybe it would lead to the emergence of other fears.

But it was better to have in the back of her mind a bit of terror if it could help get her back to normal.

#

The afternoon began; the sun with its light blinded everyone who wanted to go in the yard. People were taking a break on the porch. Even animals remained lying next to their owners, calibrating movements so as not to produce too much heat.

Martina knew this afternoon was marked as the beginning of punishment; she had cried for most of the morning. She watched the broom closet with terror, thinking of the two hours that she would be locked up.

How long were two hours? Longer than the time in which they usually eat? Longer than Sunday morning function? Longer than a Saturday afternoon bath? Longer than a walk in the countryside?

How she would feel; what would she see when the time came? The dark!

She had never thought about the color of darkness; she had imagined it would be black, because everything had to look like when the people die and are locked up in that big wooden box.

When the door closed in front and she heard the lock turn, she was plunged into darkness. She heard her father's footsteps moving away, and the sobs of mom sitting in the chair next to the kitchen table.

"Shut up! We're doing this for her own good!"

"I don't know, I'm not so sure—she'll be afraid down there!"

"Do you want try another way? Tell me what, then! If you want, I'll go open the closet!" he raised the voice.

"Sh, don't frighten her more!"

For a few seconds there was silence; Martina imagined they were talking with gestures. The last sentence that came to her ears was, "Come on, get out now!"

The dark color was not black; no other color could be compared when the last sentence faded in her ears and she heard her parents' footsteps and knew they were leaving the house.

Even the silence was not silent, but a strange noise, never heard before, dark and intense, so strong that it hurt her ears.

Keeping her eyes open or closed made no difference; the hum of the dark did not leave her. But what worried her above all, were the brooms in the back of the closet; they were used to staying in this darkness and could see everything and move at will. She felt caged under their rule.

She felt an uncontrollable desire to cry, to beat her fists against the door and scream loudly until her father opened the door.

But how much would she have had to shout before she would see him get there? And if he went really far away, no one would ever come to open the closet.

She had the impression that the room was closing in on her as if to crush her, as when grandfather passed away last year: he was closed in a box and covered with earth.

The first tear, fell from her eyes and dropped in the palm of her hand, which was trembling like the rest of her body. If only there had been a light, even small and weak—a candle—she would not feel so lost.

She had never understood why they did not want her to go out alone to talk with animals. A punishment so hard!

"How much time has passed?" she thought, trying to keep her mind away from her surroundings. It seemed like she had always been locked up.

"Soon it will open up; just think about something else…"

Instinctively she moved her legs to better settle and

inadvertently touched a broom that fell to rest on her head. Frightened, she jumped up, clinging to the door handle. The broom fell down, making a strange noise. She wanted to scream, but her voice could not get out.

She felt her heart beat faster. She covered her face with her hands and began to cry. How could they have been so bad with her? She didn't have a so serious a fault that she deserved to be locked in place like hell.

Any thoughts down here turned into horror, which she saw when she tried to keep her mind busy thinking about fairy tales.

Even the story of Snow White down here frightened her; she seemed to see the strange poisoned apple and Snow White's terrified face, like hers, full of fear. She wanted to scream and not eat that apple.

It seemed that the closet began to move, slowly sinking as had happened to her grandfather last year. And if indeed the floor was slowly going under the ground, her father would not have found her, only seen a wide hole lost forever down, down to hell. Then he would cry for his lost daughter.

The thought of her father in tears, made Martina cry even more; she had never wanted that to happen. But then, why had he given a punishment so hard, in the midst of these brooms that were soon to be leveled against her?

She felt her tears fall slowly. If only she had a friend; perhaps her friend would be out there waiting for her, maybe he would whisper comfortable words. The punishment would have been more acceptable. Instead there was nobody out there, not even one of her animals.

Fairy tales, to distract her, did not work; she had to think of something more effective. She needed to be somewhere else, run away from the darkness by moving slowly, slowly, without being noticed by the brooms, so they wouldn't realize that she was escaping.

She closed her eyes as she usually did before going to sleep, and tried to find something peaceful and relaxing for her mind.

Beyond her eyes, when they were closed, was a strange color, different from all the others. It could not be confused with the black; it was a uniform color, dusk, like a sunset when the sun is down and a red halo remains as testimony of his absence.

Into the sunset colors came another strange flash. At first, it resembled the effect of the sunset, but then it seemed to her as many lighted matches, swaying under the impulse of the wind.

She opened her eyes; the tears falling down her face gave her trouble again, and she passed a hand to wipe them off.

In the closet the terror feeling was always the same; she hastened to close the eyes again.

Even beyond her eyes nothing had changed; only the faint light was a hope. There were slow pulses swaying like a candle always on the verge of dying; their images were hard to keep in her mind, as they always seemed about to disappear.

Martina put all her strength and concentration available to keep them alive, this lightning, an unknown force, pulsing slowly.

Martina went to look for the light by thought, pushing her imagination as much as possible, focusing on the edges and on the strangeness of the movement.

"Please… come around here, there's nobody else here—it's so dark, I'm afraid."

It seemed like the prayer was bringing her close to crying; her eyes grew moist. She rubbed them with the hand dry, them, this time without opening her eyes, so not to lose focus.

Something happened—a pulse seemed to detach itself from all the others and was coming right in front of her. A flash came to light up the sky for a moment, bringing it close to the colors of the sunset.

Martina instinctively moved her head to try to follow it.

It lasted only a moment, time to catch a glimpse of a picture inside.

"Why are you running away? Don't leave me alone. Get back here!"

The light hesitated for a moment, advancing and retreating, then pulled away again, than slowly moved back up to her to wrap completely around Martina.

As a window that suddenly opens in a May morning, a bright light enveloped her mind. It lasted just a moment; the flash went away quickly, far away with all the others, accompanied by a long trail of red shades.

"Are you a cloud?" Martina said, pointing.

"You're a cloud, I recognized! One of those red clouds after a storm that never want to go away; they stay attached and awake in the night sky. You are a night cloud!"

The cloud hesitated, began to walk again, but slowed to stop by.

"You're nearby; please do not go away again!"

The cloud stopped over her.

Martina was surrounded by a dazzling light; she had to wait a while before realizing what it was.

It was the image of a meadow; a meadow with a willow tree planted near a ditch. She was sitting with her back against the tree trunk.

It was not a simple image such as a photograph, a painting. It was an image that enveloped the whole, without limitation; it did not finish in one direction but kept to the sides and behind her. Martina was right in the middle, next to the tree and the ditch. There were meadows all around.

The night cloud seemed to have disappeared or been dissolved by the great light produced by itself. Martina tried looking around, raising her head to find its nuances, but it was gone. The sky, in its place, was covered by a thick band of white clouds floating. Sometime they met each other, sometimes they separated, following a rhythm difficult to understand.

"I know, you're still here with me! Don't run away; you're just hidden in the midst of others."

She stood for a long time to see the image of the country that was still of her sitting against the willow tree. Then she wondered what to do. What to do with an image of the countryside without the scent of wind that swings the grass in the meadows, small willow leaves, the sound of crickets and all the rest? She frowned and stiffened.

It looked like a body without a soul, a thought without imagination. She felt a shiver down her back. Her relationship with the campaign was anything but impersonal. She liked to walk through the ditches with her animals. She spoke with them in the same way that she communicated with the slow and naked worms, crawling next to ditches, or with trees and planted corn.

Feeling immersed in a campaign so impersonal and static gave her chills; back there she would take in long row of trees. "Yes, I would have liked a few tall trees right down there where the ditch ends, and I can't see anything—beautiful, large trees, which then smell so much of spring"

As a call, a kind of obedience, a row of lime trees closed the view in the background like a curtain. Martina could not believe her eyes.

"But was it me?" she asked embarrassed, looking around.

There was a long line of tall and leafy trees, just as she wished. Maybe somebody was standing nearby hiding somewhere, laughing at her. She looked around carefully.

There was only her in that huge meadow.

If she was successful once, maybe she could try again. A sly smile lit up her face when she wanted the grass in May, the greenery, with daisies in the middle of the clovers.

The meadow answered, obedient, and became covered with clovers and daisies. She imagined then the water in the ditch, some trees, a bit lower, planted on its shores. She also wanted the midday sun.

She drew a long breath and stopped to look at them because they did not flee.

"How nice!" she said slowly. Her words seemed to come from another dimension; she also began to smell the willow and grass around.

"Yes, it is May!"

The image was no longer an image. She felt the desire to walk in the meadow, barefoot, on soft ground still damp from yesterday's rain.

She stood up; her feet sank into the ground; the ground, cool and moist, sneaked between the toes in a wonderful feeling.

She wanted the wind to move the leaves and her hair. She felt a soft caress on her face.

"No, not enough! I want more wind."

The grass and flowers began to move under the influence of a more aggressive wind.

"Still more!"

Martina was excited; the wind forced her head to turn away. The grass was pushed down, and the flowers bent over to touch the ground.

"No, it's too strong now!"

The wind dropped, and the grass began to sway back slowly.

"That's good!"

She also put a bird, a big-wings bird like the ones she always saw flying, on the roof of the house. Two big wings rose from one of the limes in the bottom and flew in widening circles, eventually fading far away.

"No, no. Back here; don't go away!"

The wings came back, appearing as in a movie shot in reverse. The bird rested again on the same lime tree.

"There, that's it; please, fly around here, but don't go away; don't leave me alone!"

The big-wings bird stood quietly on a branch. Every so

often it beat its wings away just a little; it always seemed ready to launch on a long flight.

Martina added more water in the ditch and put in fishes. Along with the usual gray and brown that flickered in the ponds of her country, she wanted some fish all colored like those on television.

The fields were populated by animals and plants, all those she could recall. In the meadows she also put butterflies that, obedient, appeared to stroll over the flowers.

Martina made great effort to follow her mind, trying to chase away the thoughts of being instead in the dark of the closet, under the power of the brooms. She was slowly, slowly, following her mind's thoughts, because she didn't want anyone to notice her escape.

But it was not easy to keep the images in her head fixed; often they all disappeared, and she made considerable efforts to recover them and keep them all together. Many times she had to start again the construction, as if it were a puzzle to reconstruct.

Often she could not remember what kind of animal belonged in a certain place, and she became confused. She had to put again in the water a tropical fish that had ended up on the highest branch of a tree, and then go back the big-wings bird, once again ran away.

She thought: "How did God remember everything when beginning to create the world? How did he not get confused? Not to put the snow where there is warm, the fish instead of flowers, and not to confuse men with women? He had to be just so smart!"

Another time she smiled; her eyes were now dry. She tried to recompose the images, the smells, and all the rest.

She was still tense in the effort when she heard strange noises outside her images. Her father was back and approaching the door to open it; two hours had passed, and soon she would be free again.

She had imagined crying all the time; however, she was

leaving with dry eyes and a little smiling. Anyway, she moved slowly; the brooms might notice her escape and punish her in the last moment.

When the door opened, her father's face seemed like that of a judge.

"So, you're still going to talk to the dogs?"

Martina shook her head and slipped out. Before leaving the house, she turned to look at her father. The thought she had at that time regarding her father she tried to chase it away then and throughout her life.

The first day of punishment was over; she touched her eyes to wipe away the tears, but no droplet met her hand. Hers had dried long ago.

Immediately she ran behind the house in the countryside, jumping between the ditches, looking for inspiration for the next day.

#

Martina came on the second day, while outside a storm was preparing. All day she had thought about what to do just after she arrived in the closet. Who knows if the cloud had been back there waiting for her?

She had looked into the sunset, the real one, staying long in the yard, before going to sleep. She had also sought images before going to sleep by closing her eyes and imagining being in the closet. But behind her eyes there was nothing, only darkness.

She wondered if imagining in that way was tantamount to disobeying the punishment imposed by her father. If she ran away in her thoughts it was comparable to a real escape. She wasn't sure, but the fact of her not having spoken with any dog made her quiet.

She went into the closet closing her eyes, hoping to escape right away.

She sat down, crossed her legs, and waited until her father was far away, than put her head on her knees, clasped her head with her hands, and closed her eyes. She tried not to think about the fear and immediately pushed her imagination.

The night clouds reappeared without any effort. No need to call, the same cloud came forward slowly, gloating just a little.

She found herself sitting, her back against the willow beside the ditch.

She restored the lawn, the long row of lime trees, the big-wings bird, the fishes, the wind, the sun, and everything else. She explored every corner looking for imperfections to be changed, but it was the way she wanted. She had managed to build a lot faster than the day before.

She stood in contemplation for a long time, until the effect seemed to vanish, like a beautiful song when, after hearing it for a long time, it slowly begins to lose its charm. Like a book read several times or a painting that time turns invisible.

She felt the darkness of the closet nearer, the brooms now next to her thoughts. They had noticed her escape.

Martina began to tremble; there was something that was not working, but she could not understand; her mind seemed to lose strength. Even the images seemed to sway imperfect in the fog.

She looked up to the clouds flowing always in the sky, and saw how its blue changes color into many different shades. Every now and then the sun hid its rays, depriving the land of the most beautiful, but always popped up as a surprise, a funny joke.

She stood up, crossed the ditch, and kept to the shore, her head bowed down deep in thoughts. She passed the row of plane trees, to the tall trees where even the big-wings bird was perched. She came back and sat against the willow. Then she got up and stood a long time, watching the clouds.

"Now I need a friend," she said slowly.

Martina never had any real friends, perhaps because of her unfamiliarity with their games, but she had never felt the weight of loneliness.

When they were playing with cardboard houses and dolls, she looked at them with wonder, unable to understand how their imagination could be limited to imitate the adults: a house, a kitchen, a hall, a garden, and the dreams about boys.

She instead put immense forests full of animals and flowers. The rivers flowed down from the mountains after having flowed from the glaciers.

She could see the sea and a long line of trains running on the prairie, raising clouds of dust under wide-open skies and the green hills.

Her friends remained silent when she fantasized, winking to each other ample nods and smiles of understanding and compassion and waiting for the end of her stories to softer fantasies.

"Yes indeed! Now it would take a friend!" she thought, still looking at the sky.

"He would be here talking with me beside the willow. Perhaps I would add a few trees, have a competition to see who finds the most beautiful cloud."

She sat back against to the willow tree, watching the clouds flow. It looked like a big world that had been attacked in the sky. It was like that time in the city, when she had risen in the elevator of a large building with her mom. From a balcony she had watched people walking in the street like little ants.

It had seemed a different world.

"I wonder if they also do the same thing with us, watching from up there."

She pressed her back against the tree to sit taller and present herself better to their looks. Maybe there was someone like her looking down, dreaming of a better world.

"There's a whole world up there, so great. I wonder if

anyone's looking for me…"

Martina scanned the sky, at first incredulous, but over time the search became stubborn.

"Where are you? Show yourself! Don't be shy…"

She looked and smiled a little for to show she was joking. But the dynamics of the clouds could not keep the reference; the sky changed too often.

Then she decided to fix only a small portion at a time; she focused following any change to the color and shape of the clouds. The clouds increased volume then became smaller; sometimes they was aggregating, sometimes separating.

She turned her head several times in concentration up to dwell in a small vertical space just above the willow.

To scan better, she was forced to let slide back along the trunk of the tree, almost lying on the ground.

"There you are! I found you!"

It was a little lonely cloud; none of the others seemed interested. He was walking in the sky, sometimes white, sometimes gray, till becoming beautifully dark. When he found a free portion in the sky, he then stretched into a long white stripe.

The sun did not disdain to spend time too close, sometimes hiding behind him, bringing out his profile; he let it show through.

"Here, it's you! You're like me!"

She stood up, pointing in his direction. She looked and smiled.

"What are you waiting to come here? I can't bring myself to go up to you!" The cloud stopped, uncertain.

"Don't be shy, I just want to play with you!"

He had a flicker, then went down slowly like a feather on a breezy day, or as the mist when it falls from the sky and stops along the ditches. He was leaning against the top of the willow along the branches, dripping to the ground as rain, a strange rain that does not flow but accumulates in height.

Martina followed the evolution with a smiling face and was a little bit worried. In front was built a transparent image, a child, as big as her, looking straight into her eyes without seeing.

Martina was uncertain because the child appeared to be asleep, locked in another dimension. She did not know if calling him would wake him or hurt him.

Walking slowly, she took him gently by the hand and put her mouth to his ears.

"Will you play with me?"

The child seemed to hear her after a spell.

He looked into the countryside, his brows furrowed in worry; he turned his gaze to her.

"Hello, my name is Martina and you are?"

The boy looked at the girl, then the sky where he had come from, then the ground on which he rested his feet; then smiled.

"I don't know my name; no one ever calls me!"

Martina laughed and stared at the boy in front of her.

"Really, don't even call me so much…"

The child examined his own body, moving his arms and legs and touching his head.

"But who am I? Where did I come from?"

Martina pointed to the portion of the sky where he was just a moment before. The child looked up at the sky, then turned his gaze back to her.

"It's there I come from?"

"Yes, there is. I called you," Martina said, smiling and a little red with shame as she saw the child's genitals. The child saw her blush and was amazed.

"Why did you turn red?"

"Here we must cover those parts!"

"Really?" said the boy "Why?"

CHAPTER TEN

On the third day Martina had anticipated her father, she decided to stand in front of the closet before the usual time. She was anxious to get inside, but her eyes showed the same suffering; she did not want too much tranquility to induce her father to change punishment.

But she was in a hurry; under the willow tree was a friend waiting.

There was no other way to go back to him except through the closet. She had tried in every way to imagine the same willow by focusing, but failed. She had tried in the dark of the room, but was not the same dark and imagination could not take her away.

There was something magic and special in the closet if a place so desolate was able to raise the mind. Perhaps because she had overcome her fear inside there fighting for a long time and her mind had found the strength to escape.

She had tried the night before in one of the most beautiful starry skies she had ever seen. The afternoon thunderstorm had cleaned the horizon, and the stars seemed to hang just above the roofs of the houses. She had felt a sense of abandonment and happiness, but her mind remained empty of images—if she closed her eyes could see nothing but dark, vague, and indefinable images.

What she could invent in the closet, was unrepeatable anywhere else.

#

As the door closed and the key turned in the lock, Martina relaxed, sitting up. A thrill of happiness ran down her back; she had never imagined being so comfortable in the most terrible place.

She closed her eyes, and the images were composed as they had always been in her mind.

The countryside took her immediately, even more beautiful than the day before. Her smile lit up her face as she approached to meet her friend. Together they walked along the ditch up to where it had never gone before.

Deep doubts agitated her friend.

He did not understand what had happened; there was nothing in his memory. He tried to remember, but it was useless; he did not remember anything in the world where he was before or even this one.

There was a void behind him—the feeling of being alive just from the moment he heard her voice.

Martina told him about the people who lived in the small town, her family, other families, dogs, cats, all animals, and the countryside where she was. She confided to him that at the same time they were talking about, right now, she was somewhere else: locked in the broom closet. She was keeping her eyes closed just to be here with him.

"How do you do it?" he had asked incredulously. "To be there and here with me at the same time? To keep your eyes closed in the dark and be here in the sun just standing with me and talking?"

Martina smiled with a shrug. "It is not difficult! When I

close my eyes I'm here; when I open them I am in the closet."

She wanted to explain better, but she could not understand just how it happened. It was hard the first time, but from that moment it was quite natural.

The child listened intently; it was too difficult to understand why his new friend suddenly, as following a strange command, would go back to disappear into another world, far away.

"Why can't I come away with you once? I would not bother you; I would be good."

"You can't come with me, because when Dad opens the closet, I have to open my eyes, and everything disappears. I come out from the closet, and you stay locked inside."

"Locked inside?"

It was even more difficult to imagine being locked in a closet, while the sun was so bright that he could not keep his eyes closed for more than a few seconds.

"How can I be locked inside?"

Martina did not answer, she shrugged her shoulders, as she did not know, either.

"So if one day you will never go in the closet anymore, I don't see you anymore? What will happen to me?"

To this question Martina had no answer.

#

Martina chose the name for her new friend: Edward, the same as another child who went to school with her, the only one sometimes she had enjoyed, before losing him due his family moving to another city. She shortened just a little the name because it was easier to say: Edi.

"Really? I come from there?" asked Edi.

Martina smiled, pointing where she had first seen him. "You were at that piece of sky above the willow, then you rained down!"

Edi looked up, then to her.

Martina was happy next to Edi; she finally had a true friend. She was sure he would not have betrayed her and never would have laughed at her imagination, but she was worried about the question: *What will happen to me if you don't come in the closet anymore?*

She realized that had an obligation when she had decided to do it down here. He was not a toy to be left in a corner when it wasn't fun anymore.

"Are you glad to be here with me?" she asked stopping the walk and looking into Edi's eyes.

"Of course I'm happy to be here: why do you ask? I want to learn how to live, what to think to be happy. I want to know the lawns, plants, animals, and all on the earth. If one day I should be alone, I want to be able to handle it the same. One day you will get tired of me: I want to know as quickly as possible what it means to live, how do you—"

Martina stopped him by taking his hand; continued to walk.

"It will not happen that I get tired of you—don't worry. But then how can I make you know the world if I don't even know it? I am confused, distracted, and I can't put things in the right place. I also hang the fish over a tree—"

"If your imagination was so strong that it brought me here, it will just be able to make sure that I know the world. It does not matter if you confuse things; if things I learned aren't not exactly the same as everywhere else, I'm sure it will be very nice, maybe even better!"

Edi smiled, Martina instead thought of her situation, her failure to take the place of God and create a world without confusion. What would have happened if she had forgotten to put in the world the rain or Christmas? What would the world be without a Christmas?"

Edi felt his friend's worry.

"Even God got scared when deciding to create the world; maybe he did it the same way you did. You are my

God: I have to trust you; if you want, you can make me happy or sad just with a thought. You can make me alone or take me in your hands. I'm happy when you're here with me. Far away, I don't know what would happen, I don't know the world, I could vanish into the air…"

Martina was confused. "No!" she said decidedly. "It will never happen; I will not abandon a friend!"

#

Martina could not sleep that night. Throughout all the afternoon, after emerging from the dark closet, she wandered the countryside in search of a solution. It was not so easy to do as God did. He, despite being perfect, had taken seven days. She had already wasted three before putting just a little lawn, a big-wings bird, and a weeping willow.

She could never do such a difficult task as create a whole world. That would mean inventing things she didn't know, far from her imagination.

She felt the responsibility of taking the place of God, to have the awesome power to bring Edi to smile or cry, to bring him life or lead him to death. No one can feel like God, she thought, certainly not her.

She would have been wrong, confused the mountain with the sea; her thoughts would melt, driven by fantasy, in a series of errors and the world would be neither real nor ideal.

What would have happened to Edi after the seventh day, when she no longer was able to enter the closet?

She regretted having taken such a responsibility, brought up a new life out of her own selfishness, just to battle a little fear of the dark. She could never bear to hurt him. She had always been apprehensive about any animal suffering; even in the fall, when she saw the leaves turn yellow and dry, she suffered for them.

How could she imagine if one day Edi had vanished

just because she had not been able to meet him?

In the dark of the night, Martina could not get to sleep. She didn't not want to accept this responsibility; she felt compelled, surrounded.

Finally it was just imagination, she thought, the day after entering the closet, she could turn the page, change the game, and imagine being somewhere else—perhaps at sea rather than on the meadow next to the willow—and restart without bringing other people.

There would no longer be Edi at her side to remind her for her responsibilities. It was just four days more and then the punishment would be over; she would return to normal life, and, over time, it would be forgotten that she had responsibilities like God's.

Martina got out of bed and went slowly to a chair by the window and watched the sky over her home. It was clear; just some flash in the distance lit up the sky occasionally coloring it with strange and fleeting shadows. Above her head the stars seemed to be competing for which one emitted more light.

"As God..." she thought. "But will it not be sin, to think of being like God?"

Martina was concerned: she did not want to sin, but what was wrong thinking about life as beautiful as possible for a friend? She wanted to enable him to live well. She certainly would not have felt uncomfortable if she'd been born with a better life and many close friends.

She could create many nights even more beautiful than this and sit outside and watch the stars and not behind a window, without the fear of someone seeing her and screaming that she return home.

Martina got out of the chair and ran back to bed, getting under the sheets but sitting up, with her arms resting on the pillow and her head supported by the hands.

She was shivering and thinking of when all would be finished on the seventh day and the promise she made. Edi's life hung on a promise.

What would have happened to her friend?

She must strive at all costs to build a true world for him. She had to ask a little help of her memory, to bring to the front of her mind the postcards, newspapers and television, even her grandfather's old stories.

She could not get to sleep and probably lay awake all night, alternating joy for a task so beautiful and important, with fear for a responsibility beyond her possibilities.

In the end she decided not to hold back; she would do her best and would build the most beautiful world she could imagine for her new friend.

#

The next morning she showed agitation out of the ordinary; the mother also noticed and asked her what was going on, if all was fine or if she had any problem. Martina avoided confessing her secret or she would certainly not be permitted to enter the closet; they would find another punishment.

When her father came to open the closet door, he was not entirely sure he'd been doing the right thing. He was convinced there was something strange in his daughter's attitude, the ease with which she entered the closet. When she came out, she looked like she was back from a sightseeing tour.

But he could not refuse to open the door; he would lose his dignity.

Edi was just behind her closed eyes, waiting anxiously. Today was the big day: his life would begin to flow.

Martina was concentrating and determined to not have second thoughts; decisively took Edi's hand. "Let's start now!"

Edi smiled, squeezing her hand even more.

"I wish this meadow was not as smooth as now; I would like it a little roughened, with small hills like freshly baked bread, nice loaves around which turns a white-pebbled road just around there…"

There appeared low and soft hills, rounded with care. Patterned one against the other like waves of the sea. A white sand trail started from the willow and turned them around.

"Down there, I want a forest as those in the mountains, with many tall pines, as high to almost touch the sky…"

Edi looked at the pines; for the first time, he saw a forest and trees so tall. "How beautiful! I like the pines!"

Martina pulled him by his hand. Edi kept looking at the forest.

"Let's go! Don't you want to see the wood up close?"

Together they walked, circumventing the low hills. Edi looked around with his mouth open. He touched the grass on the hills, testing its softness. The wind slowly swung the higher grass.

The wood was a dark spot; the sun was able to get into the few spaces left free from the branches to illuminate the ground and the bushes around.

When they were on the edge of the wood, Edi slowed down, hesitating; Martina returned his pull on the hand.

"Come on; what are you afraid of now?"

"It's okay to go in there? If trees fall on us? So big, they will hurt—"

"Don't be afraid!" Martina pulled him by the hand. "There are the roots planted in the ground; down to the bottom, they are strong enough to hold up the plants. Don't be afraid; we'll not take it on!"

Edi was impressed by the dark in the wood; he had never seen the dark before.

"So come on, what are you waiting for?"

"There's no sun there!"

Martina smiled. "Yes, there is some dark inside. But you don't know the dark? It wasn't dark last night?"

"No! There has always been the sun," said Edi promptly.

"Don't worry, the darkness does not hurt; it bring just a

little fear, but it does not hurt! When the evening comes, and the sun goes away, it is even darker than inside there," she said, pointing to the gloom of the wood. "But it happens so we can see the stars. If the sun does not go away, we could not have imagined the stars existed"

They went inside the wood together, leaving behind the green hills. The gloom received them. Edi immediately appreciated the fresh feeling.

"It's nice here!" he said looking around.

"Sure, but it's too quiet! I want animals, so many animals! I want the birds flying over the tops of pine, many squirrels playing with acorns and throwing them or hiding them in holes of the trees."

Martina did not have time to realize how acorns could not fall from pines before they were immediately targeted by a hail of acorns launched from a group of squirrels. They throw some, then hid behind the trunks of the trees to reappear shortly after and throw more.

Edi laughed; Martina, confused, took shelter behind a tree to avoid the rain of acorns.

"You see, I have already started to go wrong!" She was irritated, resting her hands on her hips. Edi continued to laugh as acorns rained down.

"No, I don't want so many squirrels throwing acorns!" she shouted into the forest, the strange rain stopped suddenly.

"Only occasionally some!"

In the silence only one acorn fell in the forest, and it came to hit right Martina in the head, making her friend laugh more. Martina, after a few tries to get serious, laughed herself.

The calm returned in the pine forest; only occasionally they heard the hiss of an acorn thrown in their direction from a squirrel a bit more enterprising than the others.

Over the tops of the pine trees flew a lot of birds making loud noises, calling to each other.

At the edge of the forest other animals pastured, eating

the grass of the soft hills. She was not sure at all to have reproduced them correctly.

Martina remembered the mountain forests and streams of fresh water. A little stream would just be fine there.

Both approached; Martina took some water from the palm of her hand and offered it to Edi. "Drink; this is good water!—I made it myself!"

#

For a while, they stood in the forest walking and running. Edi tried to climb a pine tree, but soon he had to give up; the trunk was rough and sticky. The last few meters he ran downhill emitting cries and making Martina laugh. His hands became sticky with resin. He ran to the stream, but, even after washing his hands, the resin would not come off.

"Really; you don't know anything!" Martina was sitting on a rock beside the stream while Edi was still busy taking the strange substance off his hands.

Edi also laughed.

Out of the forest Martina wanted a great mountain. "I want the winter up there on that mountain, completely filled with snow. When we want, we can go up there to play with the snow. When the days become sad, we can just sit and watch the snow fall, slowly whitening the ground."

On the mountain the snow began to fall slowly, with small flakes. The wind seem did not to want to ever lay on the ground. Edi and Martina flew to the high pastures like butterflies when they open up their wings in their first flight.

"How nice!" Edi watched with wide eyes. "We go up there one day to see the snow?"

Martina nodded with a smile. "Of course we'll go!"

The smile faded soon; perhaps there would not be time enough to go up there—but however, there could be no sad thoughts in their game.

"It's so beautiful, the snow, because then comes Christmas," she said inspired. "If we get lucky with all the snow on the ground, on rooftops and on the trees, then we can run out, play building snowballs and big snowmen."

Edi's eyes had widened, imagining games so much fun.

"When Christmas comes, they're all good, more than your birthday. Dad and Mom look at you differently; then you're sure they love you."

Martina spoke carefully, enunciating the words as a prayer.

Edi looked at her, not understanding, but he was driven by the emotion from her thoughts; the image of a night different from any other—a special night.

On the mountain the snow was falling in open contrast with the summer there, close to the forest, with the squirrels and birds. The sun, closing one eye, avoided sending the heat in the direction of the mountain, letting down the flakes without their dissolving.

Martina had misgivings; she stopped, tensing and clenching Edi's hand.

"What's the matter?" he asked.

The girl felt lost and looked at him.

"I'm doing it all wrong, I knew it! Can't put together all the beautiful things. The snow can't be together with the warm sun, the acorns with pine, the willow on top of a hill. Sooner or later, the snow will melt, and the willow will suffer and die. The snow is nice because it comes after the summer and the summer is nice because it comes after the winter! This can be confusing!"

Edi smiled kindly.

"I don't see the willow suffer; indeed, it's fine. Even the snow is not melting—look!"

He pointed his arm towards the snowfall that in the meantime had become abundant. "Can't you see? The sun is not looking that way, and the snow doesn't melt. Don't worry, the willow will not die and the acorns will continue to fall to the ground even if the pines are not their mothers. Don't worry, I like this world, really!"

Martina felt relieved, looked again toward the mountain, smiled, and closed her eyes, concentrating. "Now the hills begin to fall faster, so we could not imagine what there is after and need to run to find out."

The hills began to descend slowly to suddenly hide each other; the wind rose from the valley to the mountain, waving the meadow grass.

The two children began to run breathlessly, and they jumped into the grass shortly after, exhausted. Martina stopped for a moment to invent and breathed deeply, relaxing; they sat watching large open spaces, all waiting to be filled.

Martina thought how bad were the blanks, to open one's eyes and see nothing: no image for the eyes, no music in the ears, no ground for walking.

"I want there to be a huge plain to lie down on, as far as the eye can reach. Like those of the cinema—and the horses will run back and forth raising the dust in the middle of the dry earth and thorny bushes, where the sun is so hot that you never stop sweating."

An immense prairie lay before their eyes, without end. Edi was amazed and perplexed. He looked at the prairie, the horses running in big herds, raising clouds of dust that the wind scattered away.

"Indeed there is such a place?"

"Somewhere I saw it, and now it is here also!" said Martina, satisfied. The prairie was immense; the eye had wide-open spaces to explore.

"I want to be there other mountains in the background but lower, so we can barely see them. So if one day we decide to go there we don't fall down—"

"Fall down where?" asked Edi, a bit worried.

Martina paused, thinking about his question.

"I don't know; usually where there are no protections

there is the risk of falling down. But we put the hills as protection in front, so we don't run that risk!"

Edi nodded; he was satisfied.

From the prairie rose the strong smell of dust; the wind brought that together with the scent of big yellow and red flowers grown from dry bushes.

The two children deeply inhaled those perfumes. Something in the prairie wind was making strange games—creating vortices near some bushes and raising some dust to form a small tornado that spun a hundred feet before disappearing only to reappear a little later in some other corner of the prairie.

The children followed the games of the wind, competing to see who first identified the next vortex formation, pointing with outstretched arms the precise point and screaming and laughing.

Then the wind stopped playing; Martina looked around.

"Now, however, lacks a very important thing. We need a house! There you'll go when outside it's raining, or a strong wind blows. You need a house, and we'll put it right in between the mountains and the prairie, so you can go wherever you want without having to worry which is more distant, the prairie or the mountains. I want to build right there!"

She pointed to the exact place where the house was to arise. She described a wooden house such as on the mountain but with the shape of an old farmhouse on the plain, to accord with both landscapes.

She create a nice courtyard outside with a wooden fence to demarcate the beginning of the prairie and a nice porch to sit outside even when it rained. She divided the house into two separate portions: one for eating and playing, the other to go to sleep.

"So if you invite some friends, and some of them want sleep, they can go to sleep without being disturbed."

Edi nodded for so much wisdom, but could not imagine which friends she was talking about.

The two children sat in front of the house; Martina felt she forgot something but could not figure out what it was. After a few seconds, she finally realized the kind of lack. "Missing somebody! Sure, somebody to take care of you! You can't get meals, clean clothes, and everything else! You need someone to take care of you; you need a mother!"

#

"Do you really think I need a mother?" Edi asked, worried. He was not sure it was the right decision to have an adult by his side; he did not know how to behave with this kind of person, especially a mother.

Martina smiled, nodded to him to reassure him. "Of course, you need a mother; all children do!" she said resolutely. "And it's not just about making the beds or preparing food. You need somebody close at night when you wake and you're afraid or if you have any questions you can't answer. None better than a mother can do these things!"

Martina was serious. "Only a mother can comfort you or explain things as they are. Because there's no one else you can trust!"

Choosing a mother was not very easy. She wanted not too beautiful, beautiful moms think too much of themselves. Not too skinny; skinny moms are too nervous. A mother with a big smile that never goes out, even when she's sad as be going to cry.

It was necessary to look again up at the clouds. Martina began again sitting with her eyes upward; so did Edi.

"Do you see something?" asked Martina. Edi turned in her direction, spreading his arms to signify he could not understand. "What am I supposed to see?"

"We are looking for a mother for you; I'm sure there is one happy to be your mother!"

Both stood for a long time, silently watching the

clouds. Sometime Edi turned to Martina without interrupting her concentration. He watched her, trying to understand how to look.

"How do I find her? Those clouds all look the same; I see no difference…"

"That's not true!" said Martina "Look at the expression! Each one is different. Even if they have no eyes, nose, or ears like us. See there?" she said, pointing to a cloud a little disconnected from all others. "See how sad that cloud is ? And that one—look, how clever! Take a look at how they go around the sky!"

The child watched the clouds from the animated story of Martina, as if it were a fairy tale. When the girl stopped to continue the search, Edi called her back.

"Why did you stop? Go ahead, I like it!"

Martina smiled. "Not now; we have to try your mom! We have to understand their gaze. You looked at me in a different way from all the others, so I knew you were special. The other clouds didn't make you part of their games, just like all the other children did with me—so I knew that we were alike."

Martina ran through the sky, searching; Edi also tried to do the same, albeit with poor results.

The girl stopped, suddenly focusing on a portion of the sky. She watched carefully before exploding into a smile. "I found her!" she screamed joyfully. "There she is! I found her!"

Her gaze was fixed on a cloud a little bigger, more rounded, and slower than the others. The wind was hard to push; she seemed to say to the wind to slow down, not to get too excited. She swayed slowly, while all the others amused themselves by pushing her. They all did race to tease, but she does not get angry and did not become even a little black.

Edi approached Martina to locate the cloud, following her pointing finger.

"That would be my mom?" Edi asked doubtfully.

Martina nodded without speaking. The child looked more closely, observing the clouds contours and way of moving. "Do you really think she is?"

Martina nodded again. "Yes, I'm sure, that's your mom; now we get down!"

Edi looked a little more; he did not notice significant differences with the other clouds, but if Martina said, it had to be true. "All right, let's get down!"

The cloud began to swing and come down slowly; as it gained ground, most of the its surrounding fog dissolved. Slowly it came to rest on the roof of the farm, hesitated a moment, then dissolved into a soft November rain.

"She's disappeared!" said Edi; Martina smiled.

"No, she's there in the house, waiting for us!"

#

The two children came slowly, a bit timid; Martina, going to the door, wondered if she really had chosen well. There had been no doubt, but you never know.

They opened the door gently, without making too much noise.

A lady with a long apron was looking around. At the sight of the two children, she grinned and walked over. "Can you tell me where am I?"

The doubts seemed disturb the woman, but they were happy doubts; she seemed ready at any moment to shrug her shoulders and say, "Who cares? The memory will come back, as now it's gone."

Martina smiled, realizing had made the right decision; this woman really was Edi's mother. "Your name is Ginetta!" she said, smiling.

"Who—me?" she asked, as if it was a joke whose meaning she didn't catch.

"Ginetta! Your name is Ginetta!"

Martina hurried to say. Edi meanwhile stood on the sidelines, hidden behind Martina. The girl moved, trying to make him emerge. The child hid again.

"Come on; don't be stupid!" Martina whispered, after he had looked at the woman and still was trying to conceal himself. "He's bit shy!" she said, smiling. The woman, amused, looked at the children.

Martina took Edi by the hand; he was completely red. She placed him in front of Ginetta, so that she could see him well.

"He's Edi!"

The boy had attempted a small smile; Martina, however, was decided, watching the woman and understanding her reaction. "It's your son!"

The woman looked at Martina, then Edi, in amazement.

"Really?"

"Yes, I know" Martina hastened to add. "It's hard so suddenly—maybe it could take a little longer, but, unfortunately, there is no time! You are Edi's mother, even if you don't yet know it."

The woman smiled; inside her head there was nothing, so she gladly accepted an identity from Martina. It seemed a fairy tale.

"Edi's mother?" the woman asked smiling.

The two children nodded in unison.

CHAPTER ELEVEN

"Why are you so sad?" asked Ginetta.

Martina was leaning against the fence; she looked thoughtfully down to the prairie. She had spent carefree moments with Edi, running and playing, inventing games at the time suggested by her imagination. All around, the world she created obediently responded to her will.

They were playing with the wind on the prairie, with the squirrels to pull acorns, came even to climb up there, where the snow often fell.

More inventions and more imagination requires more space to run farther. Their desires were not limited to simple games; they wanted more—to imagine herds of horses running forward across the plain and black clouds against the sunset flashing to be frightening so the horses would feel scared and run home until they reached the shelter to hide.

Ginetta watched their games, sometimes participating in the fun and making them laugh.

Martina imagined wonderful days on the grass, rainy November afternoons to feast on sweets at snack time.

But every time Martina had to run away, her father opened the door, and she did not finish their games. She could never reach the sunset. The key turning in the lock forced her to return, as a reminder, authoritarian and uncompromising.

Martina would stiffen at the sound of a key in the lock and suddenly become sad.

"I must go; Dad is calling me!"

Whenever she said this, Edi looked at her with sadness. "Will you be back tomorrow?"

The girl smiled, opening her eyes in the closet; the smile remained suspended on her face even as she crossed the closet threshold and emerged.

The father looked at her, amazed and in doubt whether Martina being looked in the closet was enough of a challenge. What did she find so funny in that dark closet, in the midst of the brooms? There was nothing there to stimulate her imagination; there was no reason for her to be so happy.

He had chosen the darkest place in the house that had no distractions. Fear of the closet by now had lost its effectiveness; he had already warned Martina about the next time, that he would come up with something more effective.

Her adventure in the midst of the brooms was to end on that same day, the last day of punishment.

She was leaning against the fence, looking straight to the low mountains, so sad after having hoped already that she would not have to suffer for the separation.

Edi, beside her, was wondering what would become of his life. The thoughts and phrases intersected with each other as one big sadness of their trying to be brave without being able to convince themselves.

Maybe not all was lost. Martina probably would have found the way back; they would hold.

Ginetta was more puzzled. "It's strange! You are be able to do whatever you want: if it's hot, you get some fresh air; if you want a thunderstorm, the clouds obey you. You have built vast plains, mountains covered with snow, and you can't stop the time just for one second. Make time give us a little break," she said, letting the words come out spontaneously.

"It is not logical!" She shook her head looking away, avoiding meeting Martina's gaze. "Don't you think the time is like the snow on the mountain or the stream in the woods? Like a squirrel that suddenly, on your will, stops throwing acorns and hiding behind the tree?"

Martina began to think about the time; Ginetta was probably right, she had never treated time like any other part of their world.

How would the world be without time? If she wanted to, she could stop time. But then what would happen?

She had never asked such a problem; it was natural to see the time passing, the only means to become a woman. She wanted more time to pass in a hurry and take away the many problems of her age. She had never wished otherwise.

Imagine stopping the time; it seemed like a unnatural and dangerous prospect.

What would have happened once time stopped? If it became angry and had not wanted to restart? If, for the sake of her friends, she had agreed, how long would it stop? One hour, one day... a week?

The time would then take its normal course, or they would remain forever slave to her own world, locked up here, prisoners?

"A prison is still a prison, even if the best," she thought, shaking her head.

And if her father, unexpectedly, get into the closet while time stood still, and, seeing her in that condition, he thought she was dead? That would make the end of her grandfather. Put him in a hurry in a wooden box and thrown it away!

Perhaps her grandfather was able to stop time; he was

standing somewhere with the imagination, and the other people, not realized it, had put it underground.

She did not want to end up underground.

It was dangerous to stop time.

But if she had not done so, what would have happened to Edi and Ginetta? Alone here, with nobody to invent for them, it would not be so good for them.

Leaning against the fence, Martina was suddenly restless; she had to make a choice full of uncertainties and risks.

She had understood at from the first time that sooner or later some troubles would happen for sure. She was not smart enough to make choices; she left too carried away by imagination; her father was right.

She could decide what to do; she had to choose now without any further delay. She decided to take a break to think about it.

Edi and Ginetta immediately understood her anxiety, the look, the strange expression in the eyes before she disappeared.

She had to go back in the closet and take a break. She opened her eyes and immediately found herself in the darkest corner of the house, but now the brooms were not afraid anymore.

She had a decision to make; she needed to be alone to decide.

#

All was started here, with a little enterprising cloud, a meadow, a willow planted in the middle—and it all had arrived where she never imagined.

If her conviction was not to extend a dream that was, in any case, near to finish, she had to do it now. She had to go away at once, now, without getting caught by sentimentality. Soon her father would come to open the door.

She would come out and, in a few days, would be able to forget everything; to consider all that had passed as one of her strange dreams and nothing else!

She had no obligation towards them; it was nice while it lasted, and now she had to go ahead with her life; she could not stay child forever. What could they expect more from her?

Martina imagined them still up there, leaning on the fence, their heads bowed down. To the sad eyes of Edi, Ginetta did not know the answer.

What would happen to her friend? With no one to invent for him, without a secure life to cling to, so young and already abandoned.

It's true, she had given him a mother so he would not feel alone. She had chosen well for him; she should be quiet. Why, then, did he show such a terrible feeling? The same as in the eyes of an abandoned dog!

She felt as she had never wanted to, as the kind of person who would leave dogs on the street when they cease to be a good toy. She saw the look of a dog abandoned while the owner's car was going away; she could not forget it.

It happened one summer in the big road near her home. A car had stopped. Who had opened the door was not even get out of the car. The dog, however, was dropped jumping joyfully, sure of the walk.

The car, however, had immediately fled, leaving the petrified dog behind.

She had seen his expression at that moment—the pain and despair. She would have preferred to see him angry, growling against his owner; instead there was only pain in his eyes, as if it were their own destiny.

The dog had waited three days for the owner's return, still standing in the same place where he was offloaded, refusing food that Martina had for him.

For two mornings she had not gone to school to be near him; she had moved with compassion all the people of the area until somebody had agreed to keep him in his backyard, and he also accepted the name Martina chose for the dog: Lillo.

But Lillo never forgot that street; every time he could escape he got back to that street, sure that his owner, moved by regret, would be returned to him.

The car that hit him did not even have the compassion to stop. Martina had heard his call and his pain. All day long she kept him in her arms, trying to mitigate his pain with sweet words.

She also felt bad—how she wanted to replace his owner, to make him happy in the last hours of life, but she could not do it; nobody could.

Martina, in the closet, cried slowly, remembering Lillo. She could not behave like the owner of that dog. She had no right to give birth, give hope, and then run away because she wanted to grow up. If it was her destiny, she would meet it without causing any harm to her best friends.

It was not only a dream—a strange thought good to keep her mind occupied while waiting for her fear to calm down. She had specific responsibilities; she could not escape!

She could not leave them as long as they needed her.

#

"Why are you crying?" asked Edi, beaming at the sight of his friend still there next to them. For a moment he feared losing her forever.

"I was thinking about Lillo" said the girl. "But never mind; now I am fine!"

She raised her head and pronounced solemnly, without any hesitation: "I have something important to do and want to do it now, before it's too late."

She looked up, staring at her world like a true god.

"Time will not enter to our world! I want to see the sun

come up and stay in the sky and set without the pressure of time; only our imagination can lead its way."

She had her finger raised like Moses when he spoke to his people with the tablets of the Ten Commandments in hand. Edi and the Ginetta watched silently, full of hope.

"The morning can go on after the night, or even after the afternoon or the sunset, if we want. As on the mountain, the snow can begin, continue, or end, so even time will behave like all else in our world!"

Martina slowly dictated the new laws.

The time became thought, and could move forward, back, or stand still, following their will.

Edi could try a thousand times if he wanted, when he found himself for the first time on the floor next to the willow and Ginetta the first time that the door of the farm was open.

Her world had become like a huge lake, a huge basin of time when she could immerse and try everything that is inside: past and present, without distinction; a world where the future flows like a river into a lake, bringing ever new sensations and moments, ready to be revived whenever they wanted—always new resources to add to the other.

The future would no longer become present and then past; there would be no more regrets in her world. It would always remain present time, at their disposal to dive into.

"Even if it will happen that one day I'll re-open my eyes, and for some reason I'll find myself in the broom closet and Dad will come to open the door, I don't want you to think I am here anymore. What we feel today becomes eternal; its fragrance will never end. It will not go missing but will accumulate as a huge lake. Only the future is unknown to us!"

Martina was shining. "I will live always up here with you, and, if it happens that I can somehow forget the most important part of me, I still will always be here with you!" Having heard her pronounce a solemn oath, Ginetta and

Edi looked at her, excited. Their smiles only hinted at their deep joy.

#

That same night, the first without time, Martina felt uneasy. She was longing for the world she had left behind in the closet: her mother, her father, and all her animals. She knew that at the moment she decided to open her eyes, all would be shared from the beginning. It would take only two hours of her life.

Yet she felt uneasy.

She had built a wonderful evening: the wind warm up from the prairie flowed toward the mountain and crossed the courtyard slowly with a caress full of flavor.

She set out to go to bed, taking with her the strange uneasiness. She leaned against the window, watching the sunset.

Ginetta and Edi slept already, and a deep silence hung over the prairie.

The sunset gave its best: it was expressed in all possible shades before leaving only a red halo resting on the low hills in the background. All the time Martina was analyzing, the halo had not dissolved; it remained stuck to the hills.

Initially she had considered it just an impression. Then, as the light grew, she realized that something strange was going on.

"A sunset usually does not do like this! I have done another one of my mistakes!" The low hills at the bottom seemed illuminated by a light like so many red candles, a light swinging with all the nuances.

"I have not made up this sunset!" she whispered down the stairs toward the fence. It was dark around, a short hop to began walking in the dark in the middle of the prairie toward the low mountains on the horizon. She followed the direction of the light; the silence was not exactly silent, but a faint whisper, barely perceptible, seemed to be the same light emitting these strange sounds.

She walked toward these sounds, driven by a strange impulse. She did not know how long was her way; at the end the sky was red, a huge rainbow right over her head. Swayed showing many shades, all different.

It was her lake, just as she had wanted, a huge stretch of time, which contains images and events. Every each new event built a new cloud; it wandered through the prairie, suspended, ready to be lived again every time she wished.

Martina sat on the rocks, next to the dry bushes, watching the clouds flow.

The fantasy was mixed with real events; sometimes it was difficult to define the difference. Fantastic stories flowed together with the same semblance of reality. She was not surprised when personal events related to Ginetta presented themselves to her.

#

There was an old house in a small town. Three floors overlooked a courtyard, and a railing united many doors: one for each family. People at sunset sat and clung to the railing, talking from one to the other side of the courtyard. The clothes hanging on the ropes seemed flags, coats of arms of their rural life.

The autumn was moving more slowly this year; just a little mist could go down in the evening when the sun was beginning to lose its heat.

Ginetta was leaning against the railing, her head bowed. People were talking about her luck. Soon she would have a son.

For a long time she had been waiting for this moment, but now she was full of doubts. Her life had become complicated when her feelings were gone. Her man had stopped looking at her.

At the beginning everything was so beautiful, but it had

not been so for a long time. Now he spent the time hanging out with friends and often came home drunk. He had also started to beat her.

Her romantic dream turned into a nightmare. Every night from behind the window she spied on his face to understand his mood—to know if she had to prepare for the slap, or if he was so drunk as to fall asleep before he got to the bed.

How could she hold this child in the way, conceived in one of many nights back from the tavern, drunk and full of smells. How long before she could not feel anything for her man? By now she had forgotten what it meant; she just had to pretend so to not punish his pride.

Ginetta was ready to love this child, but what was the destiny for his future? How could she protect him from his father? How many beatings would he have to take before he learned to defend himself?

Ginetta hugged the railing, with her eyes turned down; sometimes she rose again, answering to the people's smile. She thought of how many of them had the same problems, behind the smile, hiding a sadness and despair like hers?

She wished to look up and tell them how it feels to live a life in this way. Scream her anger, without keeping it inside. They would have comforted her, showing her love, or would take her for crazy, agreeing with her husband's slaps? They would have waited until the end of the outburst to pretend that nothing had happened?

Maybe she should flee—hide herself and her son for life, but the world was as scared as much as her husband was. She would never had the courage of such a choice.

Then there was nothing else to do but wait for old age and hope that advanced years finally gave a bit of peace.

Ginetta was crying silently, with her head bent forward, did not even have the desire to lift to smile.

Meanwhile, the evening flowed slowly; someone started to return home, moving away from the railing as the dead leaves from the trees in autumn. Poor lights went on in the house.

#

The small Martina was horrified frightened by emotion so sad, she was crying. How could be great such despair? For the first time she had a similar sadness, a fear in adult mind.

She paused, terrified; she had always thought that growing up meant to be freer, larger, and stronger than any fear. Instead she saw that woman more terrified than her before entering the broom's closet.

Even her prairie had another image; it exuded sadness all around. The light had turned red halos everywhere, as if the woman was now there to despair, as if the home of her heart was right there between the prairie and low hills.

More clouds came; driven by a strange instinct, they continued the narrative.

Just then arrived the spring; the fields were changing color; the green would soon cover all the meadows.

The war had just ended, taking away a lot of people, as well as its man who died at the front. He was a hero, they said; he had long fought for their country, even giving his life.

Ginetta should be quiet and proud to be the wife of a decorated hero. But the sadness could not abandon her.

How much she wanted a little heroism, even for their family. Now would walk with pride in her heart and not wander the countryside with a dry heart, remembering a useless hero and a love lost too soon.

She had been alone, not a husband, nor a son who did not want born. There was only loneliness.

#

Martina was stunned by a pain so heavy, too heavy for its sensitivity. She went no more in search of those clouds, as she saw them reach above the head elsewhere.

Martina found even Edi's story; it was in the clouds in the middle of the prairie like a book on a shelf.

Edi lived in a small village down in the valley. Everybody knew he was a child and a bit weird. After school he never went to play with other children and did not come back at home. He took his bicycle and ran away, on small dirt roads in the countryside. Leaning the bike against a tree, he walked through the fields looking at the holes of the moles and the footprints left by animals. He climbed trees and was peering up at the sunset.

Not even a thunderstorm could scare him; he came down only with the approach of rain.

In warm weather, he went along the paths beside the railway. He leaned on the bars, at the level of the crossing, waiting for the train. With wide-open eyes looked into the train cars and the windows. He greeted with wide signs of the hands their fleeting images.

His favorites were the long trains—slow freight trains. They slowed on approaching the station. It seemed to invite him to step up and board them to take an endless journey.

Lingered long near the bars, waiting for trains, he counted the cabs.

Then the railway line was closed. The coal seemed no more interested in anyone; the gateway to the mine was closed. The trains were slowly removed, and in a short time did not pass through anymore. Traffic was diverted on the main line, twenty miles away.

Only the old stationmaster was still in place. He was no longer to receive any communication. He remained keeper of nothing, something that is no longer passed.

Edi looked over that lean and gray man, ever with a pipe in his mouth. He was always sitting on a chair next to the checkpoint.

He began to spin around with discretion. Edi hid and spied his actions. The boy wished to be like the stationmaster, to have such an important task.

The old stationmaster kept clean and shiny even if the posters and notices were dated too long ago. He got up every morning at half past four—the time of the first train—lit the lights, and checked that everything was working. He was preparing breakfast and controlling the ballast and railroad switches. After that he sat in his office, behind the large glass, lit the pipe, and looked out.

One morning, before going to school, the old station master called him.

"Hey, son, do you like the railroad?"

"Yes, sir," he said. "But it is so sad; the trains don't go here anymore."

"Yeah."

"I wonder, how many trains have you seen?"

"Yes, many, really a lot!"

The child looked at the old man as one might watch a prophet. "Really? But how many? A hundred? A thousand or more?"

"More, more, son! A lot more." The old man smiled. For every smile from his lips came a puff of smoke. "Shall I tell you how were they?"

"Really? Would you tell me how they were?"

"Of course, son; if you want you can come here!"

Edi began to go every day to the old stationmaster. He told about the time when trains were important and all the people took them. The child followed his tales dreamed of the long convoys.

One morning the lights of the old station remained off. The stationmaster seemed to be sleeping when they found him. The alarm was sounded in vain that morning. For the first time, the old stationmaster had failed to wake up.

Although the old stationmaster was dead, every afternoon Edi went to the station. Every morning before going to school, he went to check. He threw away the leaves and litter that had accumulated in the night wind.

He would sit on the bench and wait. He was sure one

day the train would pass again. He did not want the station in disarray when the passengers had come.

#

Martina spent many other nights with clouds, listening to their stories. The clouds by day flowed in the sky; at night they dozed, freeing their stories, the fantasy ones, and the real ones far away or present.

Martina did not know how it happened that she opened her eyes in the closet; her father went and locked the door. Perhaps it was a careless or sad moment. Sometimes even in paradise, one may be tired and dream of a life more difficult.

Once she came out, there was not a day that went by without her trying to get back up there. She tried in every way, by day and by night. She got up in secret to search the night clouds, but every effort was in vain.

She showed her father that she was speaking again with the dogs, in the hope of being punished. Not getting it, she prayed that the door would open; even a minute would be enough just to get back up there.

But the door did not open more, and time was stronger, erasing her memory.

A few years later, the door became similar to any other port; Martina passed it by without feel anything.

PART FOUR

...back at home

CHAPTER TWELVE

There was always a terrible smell in the alley; Martina opened her eyes, and rubbed her forehead. For the second time, the return from the plateau had a negative effect.

She waited a few seconds, the right time to compose thoughts.

Edi was no longer with her; he had disappeared as the image of the plateau, as the nightmares for more than a year had ruined her life.

She was free—finally!

Free to walk, think, and fantasize, without being put into crisis by thinking a bit deeper.

The half cigarette, was still in front of her eyes; even the syringes scattered along the alley gave the feeling of being in a place that didn't fit. She would never have had another crisis, she was sure, she had won the battle; now she felt like going home before the stench of the alley attacked her like a second skin.

She rose to her feet, swaying, her hair in her face. She wiped her eyes, still shiny, and walked out of the alley.

Leaving that awful smell, and leaving the alley for the

main road, gave Martina a liberated feeling. Before she turned the corner, she took a deep breath.

In the street, people were walking on the sidewalk. The cars were traveling slowly in a row, toward the center, on the opposite side. The wind, faster than cars, still carried pieces of paper, leaves, and small branches of trees.

The sun was still high, over the tops of the houses and over the protruding balconies full of geraniums. It gave to Martina the opportunity to wonder how long she had been locked in that alley. She looked at her watch, apparently she had spent just under a quarter of an hour there.

She slowed down for better control. She could not believe it. The lady who asked confirmation, after having revealed the time, continued to look stunned; the expression of Martina must be painful.

A quarter of an hour had passed; only enough time to make the joint, to suck and get to feel the terror—the rest had lasted only a moment.

If she revealed what happened to her friends, they would have considered, as always, that it was a blast or something like that—just one of the many strange stories that often circulated among them.

She continued walking, confused; she didn't feel well enough to hazard analysis at the time, but these hours would remain etched in her memory for a long time, and not just because it was the day her fears were gone and her mind was still being a musical instrument perfectly in tune.

There's more: it was the reason why she did not feel like screaming joyful; there was a strange sadness in her, an emptiness feeling.

She had never imagined feeling sad after such a victory. She had dreamed of this moment for a long time; she could not understand why she failed to taste it. As at a useless party, snubbed by everybody.

It was just sadness that she felt: the difference of two lives. How far from here was the plateau and the child's imagination.

It was hard to believe it was just herself who had invented that world.

She considered instead the last years: a life boring and useless, searching for a charge already abundantly present in her. She had sold her imagination to the hurry to grow up, forgetting who was before.

She was tired, very tired; she wanted to go home, go to bed and sleep.

She reached the corner of the square and slowed her pace. Her friends were standing next to the fountain and talking and laughing. Others ran, always searching for something. Should she go straight to their arms, laughing and joking, announcing to all the escaped danger? Instead she was confused, in a square, a city no longer her.

She felt an empty vessel without knowing how to fill it.

She was so far from the plateau, where she wanted to feel now—to stand against the willow tree and watch the clouds flow, or go out at night on the prairie.

Leaning on the street corner, she felt the sadness go from her heart to her eyes.

Martina cried slowly, hiding behind the wall.

#

Martina slept until the next day—a dreamless sleep, long and flat, a brief pause in life, to regain her strength. Upon awakening, she remained a long time leaning against the headboard of the bed, trying to put a little order in her thoughts

Her mother had difficulty believing her words: that, after all the anxiety, she could be quiet and there would be no more crisis.

She wanted to meet Sergeant Panebianco; she ran in the narrow streets, sure to find him. Both of them had the same job for a long time, on different sides of the road.

The Sergeant immediately noticed her face had changed; before turning the corner he had time to rejoice and hope for positive developments in her life.

She gave everyone a somewhat different version of events, easier to understand. But Martina wanted confide the truth to Daniel, challenging his disbelief. Instead of that expected reaction, he listened attentively, without showing any glimpse of a hidden expression, no elusive eyes or bitten lips.

He expressed his opinion only when Martina's trepidation, waiting for his response, was at the limit.

"I knew it!" Daniel exclaimed, sighing and shaking his head. "I knew it, could not be just an abnormal smoke effect. Inside you had hidden something important and great, waiting for the right moment to show off!" He pointed his finger at her.

"You must not believe it was just a trick of the mind. No, you're special! I've always known. You are special! If only I could have a world in my head, a place like yours, so close to the heart, so important…"

Made sweeping gestures with his hands, showing considerable difficulty defining his thoughts.

"You are so precious, to be able to move your world to come and save you in dangerous times, for it would not let you die—a world so great that it helps its creator and powerful enough to make you relive in a moment your whole life; sensations impossible to communicate to any human being.

"What do you fear about your life?" He asked, slowly enunciating the words with a look from the bottom, so close to her thoughts that she seemed to hear Ginetta's words.

"What do you fear from life, if you can hold something more important than life itself? If I could, I'd take all the time I have, all my strength to get back in that world; I would not let it run away again, lost in the memory. I would keep it close, without fear, just waiting for the right moment to return.

"Maybe everyone has a paradise like yours, but only

you can live it. Don't let it get away again!"

#

Don't let it get away again!
She had already fled. She would have enough to do just to not forget, to not deform over time: maintain the freshness that still could feel that sense of freedom beyond any other.

It was hard to accept it was not an illusion, a childhood memory pushed on with too much vehemence.

She thus accepted the unfolding of correct events, as remembered: she had been attacked and overwhelmed by her own thoughts; their strength, like frightened horses, were impossible to tame. Ginetta and Edi had helped her to remember who Martina was. For an indefinite period, she was once back again in the world imagined by herself.

Not a day passed without at least an attempt to trace the events, reconstructing images from the willow, like it was another life. There were images and moods tiring to hold because they were not in its reality. It was not like reading the night clouds; there were no emotions inside, only their memory.

It was hard to keep true to her original feelings; they came in a different way, a mirror of the mood of the moment. The images changed, overlapped, and finally fell down.

Martina came up to flex her muscles in the effort, but the images were collapsing like a puzzle that loses all the pieces. It was no use, to close her eyes and try to dispel the darkness in her mind. Behind the dark was only another dark.

Only occasionally could she rid the mind, so unexpectedly, without warning; it seemed the mischief of a child, vanishing the moment in which it was discovered.

She began to go looking for all situations that could trigger the imagination: long trips at night in the car, pushing driving out all other thoughts, listening to music, watching the few people in transit on the other side of the road with similar problems, entities belonging to another dimension.

She stopped in the side streets near the woods, lowered the window and listened to the sounds and smelled the flavors.

Sometimes she fell away just a little, until the dark impression turned into fear. During these walks, if she didn't entertain in-depth analysis, it happened that her mind was more benign and consented to travel a bit further.

She was able even to realize they were sailing without returning immediately to the ground, like one of those strange waking dreams, where one seemed to be able to direct one's own fantasies.

#

Martina had stopped going to the square, even if sometimes she went to see old friends, without revealing to them what was her personal opinion on their way of life, the superficiality in their expressions.

She no longer felt a square resident, but otherwise, not one of those people in front of the bus stopped with their scorn looks. She thus defined herself as a person in passing, without knowing what new direction was to be taken.

Daniel also had left the square, spending his time immersed in music. He played with a band, composing songs that most often ended up in a drawer. But he could not complain; he went all around doing small tours, sometimes playing before big stars, so he could also earn some money.

Martina instead found work in a newsstand. She had rented a small apartment in the suburbs. The proximity to the countryside inspired her more.

Sometimes she wondered if was a bit too absurd, desiring things impossible to obtain—if it was the time to accept her situation and her own life: a job, a boy and a decent future.

She actually did not want more; she did not want a better job, a career, or a new social position to cancel the previous ones. She just wanted a bit of her old fantasy: the plateau, the willow, and the clouds flowing. She knew she no longer had the imagination needed to build like a child; she would just enjoy a little of her perfume, close her eyes, and wake up next to a willow tree.

Knowing that, however life went, she always had something important in the heart, more than any misadventure.

She had tried many nights to close her eyes without sleeping, looking for a little light behind her eyes, but there was only darkness.

#

One day Daniel arrived breathless to Martina's newsstand, his eyes were like an owl in the dark. He was leaning against a stack of newspapers, able only to anticipate with sweeping gestures after the words were said. "I found something about you, I'm sure! We went to play in a town nearby, and I saw a house like the one told by the night clouds, where Ginetta had lived.

"We were in the square and the house was right in the side. There was a courtyard with a tall pine with broken branches on one side. A large blue sundial was painted on only one side, with a broken shaft and blackened drawings. There was also a window, the one with the old forms on the wall next to the balcony, although recently redone!"

Daniel spoke with sweeping gestures, his eyes wide like a madman's.

"What are you talking about? Those old houses are all alike! And then, you know the story about Ginetta's life was fantasy," said Martina smiling.

"No, I say, it was that! It's just that!"

She could not believe in the existence of Ginetta, but agreed to go to see the strange likeness. They decided for the next morning.

Even though she had no doubt it was fantasy, that night she could not fall asleep any time soon.

The next day, early in the morning, they were both on the car, headed in the direction of small town that was only thirty miles away.

"You'll see! You'll see if I'm right!" Daniel repeated.

The last miles they traveled silently; Martina looked around skeptically, evaluating possible references.

The place where Daniel had played the day before was a small town that, like many in that area, was at the feet of the first mountains. Streets narrowed toward the center, where a long row of houses joined together, almost holding hands. Small lanes as open cracks between the houses, like as open wounds unhealed, set off into the countryside. Large courtyards alternated, similar to each other, to reach the main square.

A church stood in the center, as high as a ancient shrine, its four wide steps leading to the churchyard. It stood with its massive brick walls, highest of all the houses in the countryside almost as a sign of protection.

Stopping the car to the side of the square, Martina looked around and inhaled deeply the country air, hoping to find some reference.

Daniel had not pointed out which house it was; he had wanted Martina herself locate it. After an ancient palace, a small alley to the countryside, the road from where they came, an old farmhouse—Martina stopped suddenly and stiffened, her eyes on the old farmhouse door.

She looked to Daniel, then again the door, and, without saying a word, moved the steps in that direction. She came anxiously, the heart pounding.

"My God! It's just true. This is Ginetta's house, no

doubt about."

Smiling, Martina stroked the stone jambs of the big, old wooden door consumed by time, then crossed the threshold until she reached the center of the courtyard. Her eyes immediately went to the balcony and the railing where Ginetta used to look out. Only the color was changed, freshly painted.

Daniel smiled.

"There is no doubt, this is just Ginetta's home! The sundial is the same, although the blue is gone now, and the designs on the hands are deleted. The tree is much higher and bigger, it's lost all the low branches. The courtyard was not paved," said, smiling with wide eyes. "There was only ground, and when it rained, puddles formed so deep that the children jumped in barefoot."

She smiled ecstatically, indicating everything by hand, and trembled at identifying new details.

"That is the staircase to the top floor; come on! There should be the first two steps of stone edges."

They walked slowly; somebody from above was watching clinging to the railing.

Martina pointed to the first two steps, ledges stone had broken away. Time had rounded the chipping.

"It's happened for the move, when Ginetta married. The bed was too heavy and fell, hitting the first two steps and breaking them."

Martina smiled happily caressing the wounds rounded by time.

An old lady had leaned over the railing, watching curiously.

"Looking for something?"

"One of her relatives!" Daniel said, pointing to Martina.

"We heard news about a relative who once lived here and wanted to come to see her old house!"

The old lady smiled curiously.

"Really? And what was the name of her parent?"

Daniel became red in the face; Martina gave him a look of reproach—what name would invent now?

"Her name was," Daniel, said narrowing his eyes. "I think she was called Ginetta!" Ended quickly the words waiting with trepidation for an answer. The old lady rested her chin on the palm of the hand.

"Ginetta!"

She smiled looking at the girl.

"I knew her; she lived here a long time ago. Who are you, a niece?"

Martina looked incredulously Daniel. The boy smiled, shaking, his head.

"Yes, she is grandson… distant!"

Martina could not believe it; Ginetta was really her name. She seemed to be dreaming and was stunned. She just nodded before looking around, then faced the thin and wrinkled old woman.

Daniel had to take her by the arm when they were invited to climb. Martina followed him without realizing it; she took her first steps clinging to him, looking again at corners rounded the time.

Strong emotions grew in her every step, strong enough to make her lose her balance. The thoughts seemed to suddenly wake up from a long sleep. She could imagine perfectly Ginetta walking on the balcony, checking geraniums, removing the dust from their leaves, and patting them as children.

It was not the normal imagination driven by a memory; it seemed that the night clouds were back, right there, over her head—ready to tell again the story of Ginetta and remind her that it was not a fantasy.

Martina saw her sad, leaning against the railing with her head down, thinking about her life and what she had believed to be a great life, living next to her man.

On Sunday, waiting for the moment to go to church, even just a few steps, close to his arm, was like walking on clouds.

Everything was done so quickly. How many times had she wondered if the lack of interest in her was due only to her fading beauty? No more walking on Sunday afternoon, no more looking attractive, a caress, or even just a question such as, *How are you?*

If she had gone, he would have noticed only because of the missing socks at the foot of the bed.

Martina was staring at something only she could imagine. She wished she had Ginetta here now, being able to soothe the pain, forget the sad moments.

The pain was too great to bear alone. What could be strong? A sadness on a sunny spring day, when nature gives its best.

She stumbled again; Daniel caught her hugging her, and looked worried; he saw her gaze elsewhere. He shook her slightly; she looked at him with inquiring, then smiled.

They stopped for a moment on the landing; something strange was going on to Martina, and his hand wrapped her hips and pulled her up, then they walked slowly to the second floor.

The old woman made to accommodate her guests on two straw chairs placed outside the front door.

She began to tell about Ginetta's life, how she lived and how her husband died in the war as a hero, how they had been a very united couple. She was sad, telling of miscarriage of her son, after the fourth month of pregnancy.

Martina heard the woman's words touch her but slowly fade away as if she were telling about another person.

Her thoughts ran fast on the true Ginetta; closing her eyes, she seemed to be back on the prairie. For many nights had unsuccessfully tried to empathize. Here, in front of the door where she had lived for a long time, there was a bridge to her world: a powerful force.

Daniel noticed. He was listening the old lady's words but, watching Martina, seemed to fall into a kind of ecstasy. Her face was enchanted. He took her hand. At his touch, Martina's smile widened and she turned toward him.

Even the old lady saw it; she stopped telling the story of Ginetta, as she watched the smile of girl.

There was a long silence.

"You really loved your aunt?"

"Just so much!" said Martina. "More than I could imagine!"

CHAPTER THIRTEEN

In the afternoon, Martina was, all time, thinking about Ginetta's house, an imagination so unexpectedly exploded. Discovering her life had created confusion; she was not so sure of the correct flow of events of the plateau, as well as she could remember.

In the old courtyard, her mind was divided: some part had followed her imagination, as were night clouds to tell the story of Ginetta, that sad life too heavy for a child's mind.

Martina was confused and felt the weight of a big fault. Like a bad god, she had given life to overcome her loneliness, then left that life as if it were an old and useless toy.

A wicked god, she was, with much power but little love and who can't say a word to comfort so much sadness. But also a small and helpless god not even able to defend herself, condemned to suffer the strength of her creation, cast out of her own world, like Eve from the Garden of Eden. She had sold everything to the urge to grow up.

Maybe it was too late. Or maybe not, yet...

Her world repeatedly tried to come to her aid. It had taken her close to death, deprived her of the sense of life, and emptied her, so she could remember.

Ginetta there helped her recover more of its past: another world, another life. It was time to address the second part of her life: meeting so much sadness.

Martina, leaning against the counter, occasionally shook her head. It was really a strange God. Maybe the night clouds would agreed to take her hand, like that same morning, so close to her world. It would have been a single bound to get there. She could close her eyes and cling to the clouds flowing up there next to the willow.

#

A great frenzy agitated her mind.

She wanted to take the car and run straight to Ginetta's small town, but it was evening—too late. She could not arrive in the middle of the night.

"Only a few miles," she whisperer smiling half an hour after taking the car and embarking on the road toward the periphery.

She drove slowly, letting her thoughts flow in her mind. The sadness prevailed, such as the impossible need to repair. What could she do? Ginetta had told her nothing during the long nights clinging to the fence. She had been too absorbed in her own dreams to pay attention to her sadness.

She wanted to know her pain better, maybe hoping that her life had ended differently.

"Just to take a look. A few minutes!" she whispered at the end of the trip, slowly driving along the road to the church.

Quietly she parked in the same place of the morning, went down noiselessly.

The small town was deep into darkness, the square lighted by two lamps placed on opposite sides of the square, near the staircase. The church, in the dim light, seemed a shadow of something more impressive.

From a bar nearby, just below her, came some noises, sometimes agitated, accompanied by bursts of laughter.

Martina sat down on the steps of the churchyard. The wind was blowing in small pulses, from the street below up toward the top of the square. It carried the manure's pungent flavor spread in the surrounding countryside.

The voices and the laughter continued to arrive strong from the nearby bar. The light from the street lamp next to the church swayed rhythmically, dancing with the wind. Martina was beyond the light cone, but sometimes, she was hit on the face, like a flash.

An intense sadness caught her. They were not the thoughts of the afternoon; something was making way in her thoughts. She looked for the reason: it was not in the late evening, in the dark, or in the vicinity of Ginetta's house.

The streetlight was still swinging, Martina stood staring forward.

She was sure, it was a situation that had already happened, but she could not remember.

Suddenly she recognized the soft call, the impulse that precedes the flow of the imagination. She received the pulse and the laughter changed in others long time ago.

It had happened so many times, just like today. Many evenings she spent waiting for her man, watching from here the door of the bar where he should emerge.

At first Ginetta had hoped it was a temporary situation, past the urge to go out to the bar and drink, which would again come back to her. But every time it always happened later, and the mood got worse.

So she began to walk at night, unseen, on the roads to the countryside, beyond the last houses, the dim lights, on a dirt road through the fields, between willow trees and bushes. A small stream in the side was the only whisper over her.

Ginetta went up to an old house at the beginning of the woods, a place called *The Painting Willow*.

It was a usual destination for all the people of the small town, especially summertime. There was a large space where children could play. At the back, uphill, a poplar wood gave way to high lime up to a source of fresh water. People, coming from the small town, brought with them a glass for drink that fresh water.

The Painting Willow was an old building in poor condition. An old farmhouse shaped of a horseshoe, accessible only from one side; in the others, only the main walls were standing. People came there for shelter from sudden summer storms.

Three big limes assured the freshness into the courtyard. Some benches were made from their branches.

The road went directly inside the courtyard. In front was spread down the countryside, a few feet below, fields of corn, clover and oats. Standing behind the fence had a small panoramic view.

The ditch that ran down from the spring was guarded from a row of willow trees with branches submerged in water.

#

There was a legend about the *Painting Willow* that popular imagination made a long time ago.

A noble knight was in love with a peasant girl and would meet her in secret at night near the source. When the father saw it, he forbade his son, already betrothed, to meet her.

But the two lovers continued to meet after the young man refused to get married to the betrothed.

They were both killed near the willows next to the source; the father of the bride got his satisfaction.

The legend saw them die beside the willows. Their blood painted red the plants. But their spirits did not go away; every night they met to be together.

None of the townspeople dared approach the weeping willows when night fell; the spirits would be hurled at anyone who disturbed their meetings.

Even for Ginetta the *Painting Willow* was an important place; there had fallen in love with her man. It happened on a Sunday afternoon, playing hide and seek. In an attempt to get first, she had clung to him, together they were rolled into the creek.

So was born their love.

So many times they met again next to the source, like the lovers of legend.

Ginetta also continued to come back every night to sit on a bench leaning against the fence and look down at the fields. Then the sadness seemed milder, less aggressive. Sometimes she felt a little happiness.

Maybe it was the image of an eternal love, that of legend, so different from her—a love that had won anything, even death.

Her love had fallen for a glass of wine.

#

Martina followed the flow of thoughts fading away; the light of the lamp continued to wobble under the pressure of the wind, looked around, and, without a specific plan, set off on a side street in the direction of the country. The same walk happened every night from Ginetta.

She walked slowly, cautiously, looking around; she could not give a logical explanation if she met somebody. But only a few small bats were flying through the trees, sometimes interposing in the moonlight, feeding on mosquitoes and moths in the corn.

A dog was barking in the distance, but too far away to be a problem.

Martina could understand Ginetta's thoughts, her anguish. She had never had the strength to listen about the night clouds, maybe this sadness was too aggressive for a child.

Now, however, it was understandable, for she proved herself during her crisis; she had seen life escape from her hands, without the possibility to dream of a future. She hoped dying would end the anguish.

After a few minutes walking, she saw a shadow in the distance: a small hill, a little more than a few feet high with woods covering the top. At the foot of the hill was the old building. She quickened her pace until she reached the *Painting Willow*.

She was incredulous at such a sight. If it was not certain of the place where she was, she could confuse it with her plateau. The shape and size of the building, the wood behind, the fence and the image of the plain beneath her gave the impression of being next to the shelter.

It was only a draft, as if some goblin had been amused to lower the mountain, change the pines to poplars, to ruin the vast expanse of prairie with a mix of corn, oats, and clover. Make it rain centuries on the shelter by reducing to an old ruin.

But the soul remained glued, and feelings, while rarefied, had the same matrix. She shook her head and could not believe such a resemblance. Her world had taken shape here, she had no doubts.

Martina walked around the yard, touching the walls, checking in without crossing the threshold. Then she sat down on a bench, looking toward the plain.

The fields were not comparable to the immense prairie; only a great imagination could have created them from normal images.

She was still wondering how it was possible that the images flowed again in the head.

#

Ginetta was sitting on the same bench, one evening, as

it was today, here at *Painting Willow*, surrounded by sad thoughts.

How much she wanted send the pain away, let the thoughts run free and close to the colors of the sky at sunset, because that would bring serene feelings.

The fiery red sunset seemed to give the plain an eternal dimension, as if she were a lot farther than a thousand feet from her home.

The war was over; the distant planes' sounds and the sirens of the city did not send their screams anymore. Many men had already returned home and were just on the fields to set them planting. After so much suffering, the country was ready to be reborn.

But today was also the day she heard of her husband's death: a hero's death.

He had been part of an adrift division back from the mountains. He had encountered a convoy carrying war and civilians prisoners to prison camps. They had carefully prepared an ambush, leaping chase through a steep path. The truck had stopped, and they engaged in a gunfight, freeing the prisoners.

But on the road, among others, her man was also killed.

A hero, he was a hero—everyone in the village said so; meeting her, they lifted their hats; women approached to comfort her and indicated her as example to the children.

"Why then I am so sad?" Ginetta sighed, sitting on the bench next to the sunset. "As sad as any other day when he was alive… I would have expected crying, despair. But now I can't feel anything: not pain, not dolor for his death. Only sadness!"

She was thinking about the death of her husband as another person, a friend or an old uncle. For too long she had been divided from his heart.

He died as a hero, saving a lot of people destined to die. Why didn't she just feel the pride?

He was a strange hero. Perhaps for great heroic deeds, not for simple gestures like saving their two lives together.

If he had put just a little bit of that courage into their life together, perhaps she would be here to cry and despair, to continue her life thinking about him, counting the days to joining him.

She would not be here to regret a wasted life, without a little sweet thought that could comfort her.

#

Ginetta died in *Painting Willow*, sitting on the bench in front of the prairie. For a long time she had wanted a little quiet.

She requested and was granted that she spend the summer at the *Painting Willow*. She would wait for the children, following their games from the window. She would prepare them a snack in the afternoon.

Somebody from the small town began to fix the old farm, but Ginetta was never able to get into it.

They found her leaning back against the bench, looking into the sunset, seemingly to asleep.

CHAPTER FOURTEEN

Martina wanted another chance, another time in front of Ginetta not only to comfort her, but for the gratitude for bringing the *Painting Willow* in her own world.

The events on the plateau, had to be revised!

Her imagination would not only create from nothing. She had also captured real events, modified and embellished.

How many more dreams were appropriate? What was the strange connection between her and Ginetta? Even Daniel, who has become a careful examiner of her life, could provide a logical explanation.

"A connection there must be, which in some way shows your lives have something in common. Nothing else explains…"

They went together, in the midst of archives, including births and deaths, but nothing seemed to intersect: no kinship, knowledge—nothing. And in this stuff, the fantasy could not help her.

What to say about Edi? What pieces of his life had come into her world? Of such stuff, dreams were appropriated…

Martina decided to find out.

She had only a few stories and some pictures from the night clouds. A small town near an old station with a line not in use for many years.

Daniel offered to help her; they consulted old maps at the general archives of the railways. With many difficulties, they did make copies of older maps with stations in the area, citing as a cause that they were researching for a doctoral thesis.

Restricting the area to be analyzed, they found an old railway branch opened a long time ago, fifty miles away from their city. It had been used to carry the laborers to a coal mine. When it was closed, the railway branch also shut down.

It was about a thirty-mile line, separated from the main route, rejoining after passing through three small towns.

Daniel offered to accompany her, but Martina refused, wanting to go alone.

She waited for the week's end for a ride.

#

She walked along an old road, passed the mountains, then the hills, deeper and deeper, until she got close to the plain. She passed the main line, getting to within thirty miles from where the railroad once passed.

In the plain, the height variations were like those of large, round boulders earth-piled, one for each farm.

She seemed to see Edi run with the bike in the countryside, to the old level crossing, lean on the bars, and wait for the train, dreaming one day to climb aboard.

The road was asphalt-covered in many different colors, patched like an old dress; it seemed the large patches were on the wounds caused by the rain.

Large poplar woods alternated with willows placed on the edge of the ditches where the water was stagnant, covered with algae and broad, green leaves.

Not far away there was a small village, surrounded by many houses of recent construction. Martina walked slowly, looking around.

The old station had become the home of a couple of families.

A few minutes later she came to another small town, so deserted and old as to make it seem back in the Middle Ages. There were a few bikes, and, on the road, an old woman covered by a black shawl, hand in hand with a child. A great, clean avenue and sidewalks well-smoothed.

Martina slowed her pace in front of the characteristic construction in which she could see the yellow of the walls. Stones and broken and consumed bricks came out from the walls. The windows for a long time had lost their fixtures, but on top of the building there still were the contours of a inscription: *Railway Station.*

She walked slowly, leaving the car next to a pitch, past the gate until reaching the waiting docks.

The building was being renovated; large scaffolds were set around the walls. The tracks were gone; in their place there were only bushes, grasses and vines.

Looking round, she shook her head. Even this was not the station where Edi used to meet the old stationmaster.

Some masons were working, producing rhythmic sounds similar to an orchestra; Martina turned to one of them: "How long has the railroad been gone?" A different voice answered from behind a window: "The last train must have taken my grandmother!"

The workers laughed together, exchanging glances.

Even Martina smiled, shook her head, and walked out of the station.

#

Out of the small town was again country surrounded by tree-lined avenues, ditches and cornfields.

She patrolled every little side street to the countryside, sometimes forwarding, but nothing else seemed to be there, outside of large meadows, ditches, poplars, and willows, all the same.

It was an impossible search. Of the thirty kilometers, more than half had been covered.

She decided to stop near a pitch; there were three large limes trees with leaves swaying in the wind. She could not resist the call of the shadow. She sat on car hood, closed her eyes, and remained to enjoy the wind.

A dirt road, starting from the pitch, forwarded through the meadows, walking around the property, avoiding ditches and trees up to a row of weeping willows beside a ditch; in the end she could see a poplars forest.

On the other side, there were more impressive trees near two old farmhouses. The roofs were ruined, and the walls, with no plaster, showed stones and bricks.

Her eyes were not yet fully closed, when her attention was abducted by a strange difference on the horizon, like a hill that had removed its top, pressed all the way down. It had an odd shape; it could look like a ballast.

She got off the car hood, locked the car, passed the gap into the country, and walked to take a look.

The trail was well looked-after, with dark earth well established. She walked through meadows and corn fields, and willow trees swollen with activities within them.

She came to a poplar wood crossed by a ditch a little deeper, and jumped on the other side without thinking about.

\#

Beyond the woods, she easily climbed the hill. There were no rusty tracks or something else that recalled an old roadbed; it was just another of the strange hills of that countryside.

Martina sat down, exhausted and disappointed, and

projecting beyond her gaze. There were other freshly cut grasses and another ditch supported by trees. Absently she followed the ditch: its curves, the parallel path unwinding. On the left was a large cornfield, on top of which protruded the red roofs of some houses. There was a village nearby, which seemed crushed under the corn.

Martina was struck by a strange feeling; she looked again at the curves of the ditch. The path, after turning around the fields, headed resolutely toward the houses after dividing in two the cornfield.

She stood up to see better with her eyes wide and her heart beating. No doubt, the image of the meadow was familiar, as that of her first dream.

There was another willow beside the ditch, probably born from the one against which she rested to watch the clouds flowing.

The woods was the one on which the big-wings bird came and went; she prayed he not run away.

She came down from the hill, running toward the tree; she seemed be back to those days.

She caressed the trunk, as a relic, and went nose to smell it. She sat down, back against the willow, looking towards the sky.

It all began here, but it was a long time ago…

There were no clouds flowing slowly, like sheep to the fold; instead, the sky was gray, and the sun was behind frosted glass. But no matter; she had found her willow and perhaps the first dream stolen from Edi.

\#

Over the meadows, walking on the gravel road, she also found the level crossing: the bars were gone—the way rose onto the ballast to get off soon after. It was the place where Edi used to watch the trains.

She climbed onto the ballast walking towards the train station.

Martina arrived a few minutes later.

Four walls precariously standing penetrates her eyes. On the ground, were piled untidily bricks, stones, pieces of rotten wood and broken glass blackened by time. Like a mountain every year drops downstream pieces of its top. It seemed ready to collapse, if only someone came up to touch them.

Her heart was pounding.

The docks where passengers were awaiting the train's arrival no longer existed; there was only the old bench, completely rusted. The wind emitted strange noises passing through the ruins, in the middle of the cracks in the walls.

She sat down on the bench, after removing leaves and dirt around the old railway. The tracks were gone; beneath her were only weeds and brambles. Some small animal moved in the bushes.

When she sat down, she felt enveloped by a sudden sadness and abandonment. This place, so ruined, without Edi was even sadder.

It would be waiting a strong impulse of the imagination, as before the Ginetta's house, her mind split into two. Instead there was an unreal calm in the head.

Remained waiting, sitting on the bench.

It was late afternoon, the sun slowly descending along its arc. There was a loud noise of insects and bird all around. Somewhere had just cut the grass, she felt the scent.

Martina was waiting...

#

She would wait for the night clouds, even if it need all night long. Would not make the same mistake again, sell the fantasy for a little safety.

The sun had set. Martina could not tear her eyes from the sky; she was glued to the bench. She hoped the night clouds would be back keeping red the sky at the horizon.

The countryside around was dark, the damp rising slowly from the ditches, the crickets singing rhythmically, the moonlight made of gray color the fields around.

Martina was looking around, hoping something would happen. Maybe Edi would be back again, appearing from the darkness, slowly, like an apparition.

In a short time, the sunset was over; no halo was left in the sky. Dark everywhere; in her mind she was getting the fear. Maybe for strange noises in the bushes or the wind whispering unearthly between the ruins, the fear grew over time.

What she was waiting overnight in the countryside among the ruins of an old railway station? Edi certainly existed, but he could not be here right now and would never come down. He had gone, kicked out from her fear, for she considered it more important to defend her own balance.

"There is no reason to stop there, and bring down the dark with the impossibility to find the way back. What I have to do? Spend the night here?" she was thinking.

A sharp noise of snapping branches came from not far from her shoulders! She whirled—nobody there. Her heart began to pound.

A dull thud came from inside the station. Maybe some animal was behind her. She let out a long sigh.

There was only darkness around, not even a little light. She would not be able to resist for a long time; she felt suffocated as the sky was pressing down, setting a deep abyss right next to the bench.

Martina began to tremble; not only for the cold and damp night. She collected her arms around her body and pressed her hands around her ears in a motion she suddenly remembered from other similar occasions.

Every time the fear was about to enter, she had always covered her head with her arms. It happened in all her own crises and even as a child in the broom closet.

The bench had become like one in the park in its first crisis, a place impossible to escape. The ruins behind, seemed brooms, ready to lash out.

To the fear call, suddenly the thoughts in her head burst, with enough power to move her head back.

At first the dark disappeared over her; the sky became gray as premature dawn. The surrounding countryside was covered with unreal light; the sun was rising slowly.

Martina, this time, without fear, did not object, she let herself go to the change of light in front of her eyes.

#

It was a wet autumn morning; the countryside seemed disinclined to wake up, and the fog kept the darkness. The sky was painted red, waiting for the sun.

In front of the roadbed two sad, rusty rails lay. From a long time, no train wheels had been allowed.

The old train station was covered with vines that came up to the roof. The windows were broken, some boarded over with wood planks. In front, on the docks full of brambles and weeds, there was a green bench, corroded by rust.

Every morning Edi came secretly to the old station.

He kept his promise to the old stationmaster: to keep it clean even after his movement, when one day he would be transferred to another station.

He collected in a corner the broken glass and removed the vines and weeds around the walls. With an old broom, he swept away the dust and leaves that covered the docks and the tracks.

They had told him the old stationmaster had been transferred away; he would not return. But something else had happened, something serious—he would not have ever gone without saying good-bye, without the latest recommendations regarding his station.

Edi would not see him again; no one would be able to

tell him about trains as he could do. They became alive through with him, each one different, just like people—from the old locomotives come forward in poor condition, limping, to the fast trains, young and snappy.

Every morning he sat on the old bench, thinking of the stationmaster's stories, then rose to return to school by bike.

But the old station degraded after every rain. The roof shingles broke, and the water flowed freely. On clear days, the wind carried away bits of the station: pieces of rotten wood, painting, an old poster with train schedules. The door creaked more and more.

Also, this November morning he was keeping his promise; he had swept away the dry leaves, dust, and litter gathered by the wind in the corners.

He had done his duty, even inside the station, and thrown away the rotten boards of the roof, wall pieces, bricks, and tiles.

He was then getting ready to leave when suddenly, from above a whistle made him look up. He had only time enough to see axes, tiles, and plaster break off and fall directly above him. He was struck violently, falling to the ground.

He lay motionless and disbelief for a long time. He did not feel any pain, with his eyes open and not even blinking.

There was a strange calm; he could not understand why he was not able to get up, take his bike, and go away. He did not want to be late for school!

He wanted to scream, but even his voice didn't came from his throat; he felt only the tears come down slowly.

Maybe he was dreaming.

Other times he had had the same feelings—felt could not move—but then woke up, and everything was back to normal. Of course it was a dream, but he did not know how to get out.

He closed his eyes, trying to go back to sleep, but

beyond his eyes was all black—just black.

He opened them again, thinking he could wake up after having slept in his bed. But in front there was only the image of the station and the roof collapsed on him.

To calm his fear, he thought the good times, to the warm afternoons when he came to find the old stationmaster. He went to get fresh water in a fountain nearby, put a whole lemon inside, and drink deeply. As they waited for a train coming again, their gaze was always toward the distant point where the rails seemed to join.

He seemed to live again those summer days, the roadbed of bushes and climbing plants giving off a characteristic smell.

He closed his eyes, and seemed to smell again the scent and catch that little feeling of happiness. The bench in the shade brought a sense of freshness. Soon would come the old stationmaster with fresh water and lemon. They waited again, and maybe the train would come this time...

He relaxed, closed his eyes. The image of the station was clear now, not that old and decrepit building that collapsed on him.

Now it was a smooth and well-maintained station. It was not even a morning fog, but a warm summer afternoon.

Finally, he was able to change dream...

He succeeded to run away just at the time when life was extinguished in him.

The last breath saw him far, far away...

#

"My God! Edi died right here! Here where I am now!" Martina was frightened. It was terrible!

The thoughts suddenly started again, flowing.

Edi was partially covered by rubble; a moment before running away, his memories were fading slowly but inexorably, slipping back like a reversed movie. Every memory disappeared shortly after being taken to memory, in a kind of countdown. They came and disappeared without leave a trace; their place was taken by a quiet calm, an attractive current could not and did not want to oppose. It seemed unstoppable, a river of sensations: the eyes of his mother, her hands, her caresses, her eyes before going to sleep, his meadows, the trees, the railway and the long line of freight trains.

The sensations did not stop even when the beginning of his life came in, ran back with other images and other sensations, together with a deep sadness that never belonged to Edi.

Martina wanted to grab the memories to understand, but their race was too fast: sudden glare and fleeting, she could not tolerate.

Then she focused her attention on the profound sense of sadness following them. She held without letting it escape, forcing the memory to reconstruct the time. Images slowed down, stumbling, then repeated over and over.

One image showed an old country road made of white pebbles at night, some houses and so much darkness around—barely discernible were an open space, a wood, a bench, and the countryside just below. Long and endless nights, full of anxiety and hopeless.

She recognized that desperation; she had tried sitting on another bench, at the *Painting Willow*, in front of the corn and clover fields.

That sadness belonged to Ginetta.

Behind Edi's life, seemed to be that of Ginetta. In a strange confusion, so strange to suddenly stop the rapid flow of memories.

#

Martina opened her eyes; the sky had turned red!
It was throbbing, sending lightning so strong to turn

away the look for not being dazzled. Even the countryside around had become red color, rocked, swinging. The clouds emitting strong impulses asked Martina to play.

"The night clouds!" she exclaimed, surprised. They had returned as in the long prairie's nights, lowering, immersing her in pictures.

But the joy of seeing them quickly faded; in her eyes was the picture of Edi's death.

The clouds, obedient to her state of mind, hurried to submit images more appropriate. They ran back in time, from the first time in the park and back to her childhood locked in the broom closet. They were almost competing, each with their own image with the same sadness, as the Magi with their gifts.

Martina accepted all them, felt her heart with nostalgia, in the same way without distinction—as sheep back to the fold, or as children who knock on the door after a long journey.

Even the three benches of sadness, from Ginetta to Edi to Martina, though distant in time, seemed the same, lived at different times by the same person.

Maybe she really did not understand her world! Maybe she did not believed her own determination, the words spoken in front of the fence, overlooking the prairie, next to Ginetta and Edi.

That time, Martina had said: "Time will not enter to our world!"

She had wanted a world free of time, where the clouds were waves of a large lake, and feelings and events were lived as they were happening right at that moment.

She had wanted the future like a river, depositing images and new emotions, and to create, in her prairie, many other clouds ready to flow and chasing; searching each other's.

The obsession to grow up had closed her mind.

She had not realized that she has become Martina coming from Edi and Ginetta. A single existence made by many lives.

It was not a family or other connections, was the same person.

The fear of the closet had expressed the imagination in the most surprising, surpassing the annihilation of the memory that each death produces. She had gone searching for emotions to overcome fear and found the past mood.

She had rebuilt, imagining them as clouds, one for each different feeling. She had not noticed that she had restored their lives by playing along with them.

"You can't! I realized that Edi was like me, but I never imagined!" Martina, unbelieving, shook her head.

"If I failed to realize we're the same person, despite having lived so long together, who knows how many other times it happened to me!" She smiled.

"Maybe it's because of the confusion. Maybe a terrible event made it such that only one person divided in many pieces and divided by time, each one different from the others, as many different colors, when combined, lead to a single color."

Her little color was up there in night clouds, in the midst of all the emotions left dispersed in time, condensed in clouds.

"Maybe one day we'll be one person again; emotions will fill, and the clouds will not run anymore to meet and separate!"

Her imagination was strong now; thoughts ran fast to every command, as strong as she had ever remembered having had.

To create it was a natural instinct, like breathing, and like any other feeling that the mind produces. She could choose at will even to create new clouds to fill the sadness. Martina smiled; she could satisfy any desire, but there was one among many, that was more urgent than others.

Slowly the new cloud began to form at the same time her imagination began to build.

It was to fill the sadness of a child, one of those easily

realizable with fantasy.

#

It was still dark around her; she remained sitting on the bench, waiting.

The station was now in good condition: shiny walls reflected the light of the moon.

The door and windows gave off the smell of fresh paint; blinds, partially closed, showed a dim light. The docks were smooth, covered with white stones to the walls of the station; no weed stood between them.

Three lamps lit around, soon to be turned off for the night. They were also waiting.

"Soon will come appearing slowly its image, from the fog it will come out breaking the perspective. I will arise and go to meet it!"

A tinkling faraway, almost from another dimension, began to disperse into the countryside. Two bars of a level crossing slowly began to sink.

The chimes went out early to leave space for a silence full of mystery and hope.

Soon it would come.

It was a distant whistle, then two sparkling eyes emerged from the mist, to break the silence awakening the asleep thoughts.

The shape of a locomotive was coming fast to the station.

Martina got up to get ready.

The loud noise and the clatter of the wheels made her face for a moment to turn away.

"One, two, three..." she counted, smiling.

"Ten, eleven..."

She had traced a mark on the gravel with the feet, shortly traced another, then another and another.

"Forty nine, fifty..."

A cab, smaller than the other, was stuck in the queue,

followed the happy group.

"Fifty one!"

She raised her arms, happy, running and jumping around the bench.

When happiness was filled, she sat down again and sighed long.

The old station was back to ruins, as well as the rusty bench and everything else. But a new cloud was added; it followed quickly, going in the middle of the other, searching other similar feelings to fill.

Martina was now ready!

There was another cloud in her heart, she tried frantically in the midst of all the others.

"Come on, come on little friend. Don't you remember me? … Come on, don't be afraid!"

It was her first small cloud of the broom closet, she found floating with the others. She came forward slowly, as was over wrapped the entire station with its light.

Martina closed her eyes and ran away! …

#

The day was so beautiful; some wind came down from the mountain. Perhaps it was spring, or only its scent, that from the high layers slipped into the valley. Large, white clouds floated in the sky like ships that were being detached from the port begin their travel slowly, swinging, an enormous flock of sheep behind to invisible shepherd. Sometimes they joined, sometimes they were separated following an instinct that Martina—Now she could understand!

She had the look turned toward the high, taken away from the dynamicity, their spell. Even her ears did not feel nothing else that slow sliding. In her head, she had been gone forming a sweet music, a unknown mental transport.

Also closing their eyes, the clouds continued to slide in her thoughts, slowly. So she seemed to be in a middle, taking part of that gentle and tender walk.

She had a joy in heart—difficult to contain, she was trying again the same feelings, with the same power.

She stood caressing the willow tree and brought back her eyes to the sun, which seemed to be smiling.

Slowly she walked the road of white stones around the hills into the woods. Anxiously awaited the squirrel pulled an acorn and drank her water.

She came out on the other side; over the mountain the snow was coming down slowly. She run till she could see the farm.

She sat down, looking at the plain. A small tornado was waving the prairie, down near the low hills. Two children were riding the wind, jumping like two young horses.

In the courtyard Ginetta was leaning against the fence, smiling and watching their games.

Martina, sitting on the last hills before the refuge, smiled with tears in her eyes; she could not find the strength to get up and go down. She was sure her legs would not stand for such an emotion.

She waited for a moment; her heart was pounding.

When she felt the strength come back, she stood up and began to descend.

"We will call together all our emotions,
    all our thoughts left dispersed over time.
    They will meet in a single moment,
    the only moment longer than infinity.
    The future time of the heart."

The End

NIGHT CLOUDS

Sometime in the Evening
You'll Fall Asleep on the Back of the Moon

Poems and Songs

I think that the intuition of a poet belongs to everyone, because it is from everyone that comes his intuition. I present things that don't know, coming from another part of me. Sometimes I think I understand the meaning, sometimes don't... I feel pain and joy, the source of which is unknown, touch on me softly or strongly, changing my vision of life.

It 'a book of poems, the first of a trilogy. It 's a journey that hypothetically accompanies the reader into his path. This collection of poems and songs reads through very much like a story.

"While there isn't a traditional character arc or journey, there is a character arc/journey filled with wonderful scenes, characters, and emotion."

Domenico Corna

Isbn: 978-1481943215
February 2013
www.domenicocorna.it